Melanie and the
Cruise Caper

The
Twelve Candles Club

9606

Melanie and the Cruise Caper

Elaine L. Schulte

BETHANY HOUSE PUBLISHERS
MINNEAPOLIS, MINNESOTA 55438

Melanie and the Cruise Caper
Copyright © 1996
Elaine L. Schulte

Cover illustration by Andrea Jorgenson.

Published in association with the literary agency of Alive Communications, P.O. Box 49068, Colorado Springs, CO 80949.

Published by Bethany House Publishers
A Ministry of Bethany Fellowship, Inc.
11300 Hampshire Avenue South
Minneapolis, Minnesota 55438

Printed in the United States of America.

Library of Congress Cataloging-in-Publication Data

Schulte, Elaine L.
    Melanie and the cruise caper / Elaine L. Schulte.
       p. cm. — (The Twelve Candles Club ; 10)
    Summary: While running the childcare program on a Caribbean cruise ship, Melanie and her fellow club members stumble into a mystery involving drug smuggling.
    ISBN 1-55661-538-8 (pbk.)
    [1. Cruise ships—Fiction. 2. Mystery and detective stores. 3. Caribbean Area—Fiction. 4. Clubs—Fiction. 5. Christian life—Fiction.] I. Title.
II. Series: Schulte, Elaine L. Twelve Candles Club ; 10.
PZ7.M3867Mc   1996
[Fic]—dc20   CIP
96-25232   AC

To Rochelle Glöege,
a great editor.

ELAINE L. SCHULTE is the well-known author of thirty-four novels for women and children. Over one million copies of her popular books have been sold. She received a Distinguished Alumna Award from Purdue University as well as numerous other awards for her work as an author. After living in various places, including several years in Europe, she and her husband make their home in Austin, Texas, where she writes full time.

CHAPTER

1

Wildly excited, Melanie Lin rushed to the concrete bench in her family's Chinese-style courtyard and began glancing through the cruise ship brochure.

A huge white ship, the *Golden Isle*, sailed across turquoise seas on the cover. Other pictures showed white sandy beaches and brilliant red and yellow island flowers.

Calm down! she told herself, but her heart didn't stop thumping. Could the Twelve Candles Club girls really be going on a Caribbean cruise tomorrow? And could five twelve-year-old girls actually take care of twenty-five kids on a cruise ship? Sure, they'd gotten baby-sitting experience this summer, and they'd learned a lot from their Morning Fun for Kids playcare. But twenty-five kids on a cruise ship?!

Melanie heard the other Twelve Candles Club girls on the cul-de-sac out front and jumped to her feet. Their voices, and even the whirring of their bikes, carried around the white wall.

"Hey-hey!" Tricia yelled. "We're going to the Caribbean!"

"Caribbean cruise, here we come!" Jess's voice added.

"It's not for sure yet," Becky warned them.

Their shyest member, Cara Hernandez, said, "It seems hopeful. After all, we're meeting with the travel agency lady in just a few minutes."

Melanie rushed through the courtyard to greet them in her white denim cutoffs and purple Tee. When she rounded the front wall, she was glad to see they'd all dressed down, too.

The four girls braked their bikes on the driveway, and Melanie glimpsed each of her Twelve Candles Club friends as if they were in snapshots.

Jess McColl—TCC vice-president, short and athletic, with cropped brown hair and hazel eyes, wearing a peach Tee . . .

Tricia Bennett—TCC treasurer, a dramatic reddish blonde with green eyes, green Tee . . .

Cara Hernandez—TCC secretary, heart-shaped face, almost black hair, brown eyes, yellow Tee . . .

Becky Hamilton—tall and sometimes klutzy, brown hair, blue eyes, blue Tee, and president of the club.

"Hey-hey, yourselves!" Melanie laughed.

She no longer felt so much like an ABC—"American-born Chinese"—with them. Besides, they'd accepted her into the Twelve Candles Club just last month. Now, if she didn't get nervous and start to jabber . . .

"We can't leave our bikes in the driveway," Becky said

in her presidential tone. "Remember the burglar!"

"I remember," Jess answered. "He was at my house!"

Melanie drew a breath. "Put your bikes behind the courtyard wall. A bike burglary is the last thing we need."

Tricia hopped off her bike. "Between the burglar and the women trying to kidnap me, I'm losing my trust in people."

"I can't blame you," Melanie answered. "Come this way. It's so warm out today, we thought we'd have the cruise meeting out here in the courtyard."

Her artistic mother had designed the courtyard before they'd moved from New York in June. The front wall gave the courtyard privacy since their house and Auntie Ying-Ying's stood on either side, and purple ice plants grew on the back hillside. A Chinese courtyard was odd for Santa Rosita, California, but her new friends seemed to like it. She tried to see the shady courtyard through their eyes: thick bamboo stalks tied under the peaked roof . . . red ceramic Chinese lanterns hanging over the long red-tiled table and benches . . . extra seating benches at the outer edges . . . a huge wok in the built-in barbecue.

Becky walked her bike in behind Melanie. "Hurray! On a cruise we'll be getting away from burglars and other bad guys."

"Let's hope so," Melanie answered. "But I doubt a cruise is just for p-e-r-f-e-c-t people."

Cara kicked up her bike's kickstand. "You mean burglars and other bad guys will be along?"

"It wouldn't surprise me," Melanie decided. "Maybe not as many as on the streets, but probably some bad guys. Dad says one out of ten people has a tendency to steal."

"*One* out of every *ten* people!" Jess repeated.

Melanie nodded. "One out of ten. Thank goodness lots of them don't give in to temptation."

Jess said, "Explain, please."

"Ummm . . ." Melanie began. "If a person with a tendency to steal sees a ring she likes in a store and knows no one is looking, she might be tempted to take it. But she has to fight that temptation because she knows it's wrong."

"I see what you mean," Jess replied. "I guess doctors like your dad know lots of interesting things about people."

"Sometimes too much," Melanie said, "and I'm apt to jabber all about it, too!"

They laughed, and she grinned herself.

"Fight temptation is what my Gramp says," Tricia put in.

Melanie nodded. Tricia's grandfather was a retired minister, and she learned lots about the Bible and spiritual stuff from him.

Cara raised her eyebrows. "You're saying there might be bad guys on a cruise ship?"

Melanie headed for the table. "That's what I'm saying." She flipped the cruise brochure pages to *Shipboard Services*. "It says under *Valuables*, 'For your convenience, the ship's purser accepts valuables for deposit in the ship's safe. Valuables such as jewelry, money, and important papers should not be left in your cabin.' "

Becky's blue eyes widened. "Let's hope we don't have that kind of trouble!"

"You know it!" Melanie said, and Jess, Cara, and Tricia echoed the same words together.

They laughed, and Melanie added, "Let's sit at the table. Auntie Ying-Ying is serving cookies and lemonade when she brings the travel agent."

"Nice," Becky said.

"Nicer than *hot* Chinese tea in August," Melanie agreed. "Believe it or not, I had to talk her out of hot tea."

"Thanks," Jess said. "But, you know, I wish I had an aunt like her instead of plain ones like mine."

Melanie gave a laugh. "Auntie Ying-Ying isn't 'plain,' that's for sure."

She glanced at Auntie Ying-Ying and Uncle Gwo-Jenn's kitchen door. Not there yet. No sign of Cousin Fender-Bender, either. Now that Connie finally had her California driver's license—after her fourth driver's test—she was probably out driving on the freeways with her friends and giving the other drivers heart attacks.

Tricia remarked, "Chinese tea sounds special."

"It's all right," Melanie answered, "especially for cold weather. But give me lemonade any day now."

"How'd you hear about this bargain cruise?" Jess asked.

"Auntie Ying-Ying knows Mrs. Wong, the travel agent, from church, and she . . . I mean, my aunt . . . is always hunting for bargains."

They settled on the benches that lined the long red-tiled table, and Auntie Ying-Ying's kitchen door burst open.

"Hello, girls! Hello, girls!" Auntie Ying-Ying called out in her choppy Chinese English. "Don't worry. We come . . . we come! Good seeing you here again, TCC girls! Exciting to go on cruise, huh?"

The other TCCers answered uneasily, maybe because they didn't know what to expect from Auntie Ying-Ying either, Melanie decided.

Auntie Ying-Ying wore a red Chinese blouse and black

pants, and looked FOB—fresh off the boat—as usual. Smiling from ear to ear, she carried a black Chinese tray with clear plastic glasses and two pitchers of lemonade.

Behind her came a middle-aged Asian woman carrying a blue-and-white plate of cookies. Homemade almond cookies, Melanie guessed, since Auntie always tried to share the Chinese culture.

Auntie said, "This is owner of Santa Rosita Travel, Mrs. Sally Wong. And here is my niece, Melanie. Melanie, you tell names. Auntie losing breath."

"How do you do, Mrs. Wong," Melanie said politely. "This is Cara and Tricia and Becky and Jess. We're the Twelve Candles Club. We do all kinds of jobs . . . baby-sitting, house cleaning, car washing, dog walking. . . ."

Mrs. Wong nodded politely and placed the plate of almond cookies in the middle of the table. "I'm pleased to meet you girls," she said without a Chinese accent. "I've seen you on television and read about you in the newspapers this summer. You're becoming famous."

The TCCers laughed, and Auntie Ying-Ying smiled as she placed the tray with the lemonade pitchers on the table in front of Melanie.

"Mrs. Wong tell you all about cruise trip while you eat cookies, drink lemonade," said Auntie. "Melanie, you help with lemonade. Tricia, you please help with cookies."

Melanie kneeled on the concrete bench to pour the lemonade while her aunt advised how to do it. She almost muttered, "Watch me spill it," but stopped herself.

Next to her, Tricia took charge of passing the napkins and full glasses of lemonade around the table to everyone.

"First," Mrs. Wong said, "I want you girls to know how

much I appreciate your filling in for the ship's childcare people at the last minute. Two staff members had to take off, so if it weren't for you, there'd be no kids' program at all."

"So that's what happened," Jess said. "My mom says most cruise ships have regular childcare."

"Yes," Mrs. Wong answered. "In any case, our travel agency booked so many cabins at bargain prices—and to people with children—that we got the cruise people to agree to our furnishing our own childcare."

Exactly what Auntie Ying-Ying had explained, Melanie recalled.

"I think you'll enjoy the cruise, even though you'll be working on the ship," Mrs. Wong added. "You won't be expected to take the children on shore excursions. So basically you'll just be in charge of the children when the ship is sailing, and then only *if* parents want their children in the childcare program. Some parents might not use your services at all."

Melanie hoped some wouldn't. There were twenty-five kids from Santa Rosita!

"Where will we sleep?" Jess asked.

"We have a large cabin for four reserved for you," Mrs. Wong answered. She turned a smiling glance to Auntie Ying-Ying. "And you'll have Mrs. Lin in the cabin next to you if you have any problems or feel the least bit homesick. Melanie will share her aunt's cabin."

Right, Melanie thought, *along with my ten-year-old brother, William, and five-year-old sister, Silvee.*

Melanie glanced up at the second-floor windows of her house, almost expecting William to be looking down and planning mischief. As if his endless karate chopping and

"Hiii-ee-yah!" yell weren't bad enough! Luckily, Mom had taken him and Silvee out clothes shopping.

Becky asked Mrs. Wong, "You think there'll be other kids besides these twenty-five from Santa Rosita?"

"I doubt it," Mrs. Wong answered. "School is starting for lots of children in other parts of the country. Not too many will still be on summer vacation."

"Let's hope there aren't other kids to take care of!" Melanie exclaimed, still worried whether they could handle such a big job.

"I'm impressed with you girls, and so grateful to get you at the last minute," Mrs. Wong said, changing the subject.

As for "last minute," Melanie thought, even Auntie Ying-Ying's going on the cruise had come about just a week ago. Others in Santa Rosita had learned that the *Golden Isle* had lots of empty cabins, which meant last-minute bargains. Uncle Gwo-Jenn wanted to stay home, and Cousin Connie was returning to college.

Mrs. Wong handed out cruise brochures. "Besides babysitting, you'll be expected to help make kids' costumes for costume night, take them on a tour of the ship's bridge, accompany them to kids' movies in the ship's theater, and all kinds of other activities."

She added, "The ship wouldn't have a youth program next week if you weren't doing it."

Melanie asked, "Do you think we can really do it all?"

Mrs. Wong smiled. "According to your aunt, you girls can do anything."

"True!" Melanie's aunt declared proudly. "True! Twelve Candles do anything! Girls work so good."

Embarrassed, Melanie clapped her hands to her face,

then laughed with the other TCCers.

Smiling, Mrs. Wong stood up. "Any questions, girls?"

"Will we have all of the kids at once?" Melanie asked.

"I'd guess you'd rarely have all of them at once," Mrs. Wong replied. "Maybe for costume night."

"Should we bring our clown outfits for the talent night and costume nights?" Becky asked.

"Good idea," Mrs. Wong replied. "A very good idea for entertaining the children, too."

"And maybe bring Chinese dragon outfit?" Auntie Ying-Ying suggested.

"It's too big," Melanie protested. "We couldn't fit it in a suitcase, not even in a trunk."

Auntie Ying-Ying sighed. "True. Dragon is big."

"Any other questions?" Mrs. Wong asked.

Becky asked, "Do we take arts and crafts materials?"

"No, the cruise director says they have a good supply of arts and crafts materials," Mrs. Wong answered. "They keep them for their usual kids' program, and for adults to make costumes. You'll need to have parental release forms filled out, also the personal information papers. And don't forget your passports, or if you don't have one, your birth certificates."

"Birth certificates?" Tricia asked.

Mrs. Wong smiled. "You'll need identification, and I assume none of you have a driver's license yet. . . ."

"Not yet!" Becky answered, and everyone laughed.

Melanie felt numb and excited all at once, and the other TCCers looked as if they did, too. It would be an exciting adventure. She and Jess were the only ones with passports, and even they hadn't traveled that much.

"Excited, girls?" Mrs. Wong asked them.

Tricia began to bounce up and down again, and Melanie felt like bouncing with her.

"Yes-s!!!" they all replied.

———————

When Mrs. Wong left, they scanned the colorful cruise brochures. The pictures with passengers in them were all of grown-ups. No pictures of kids, so maybe they didn't always encourage kids on this ship.

Cara asked Melanie, "What clothes should we take?"

Melanie shrugged. Lately they asked her clothes questions because she'd modeled in New York before moving here.

"I've never been on a cruise myself," Melanie answered. "I'd guess just regular clothes. Probably no cutoffs or old, grungy stuff."

"What about formal night?" Cara asked. "I don't have anything formal. I don't even have anything good for semi-formal nights."

Melanie shrugged. "We'll just have to take our nicest dresses. You know, like a party or Sunday dress. From what it says in the brochure's 'travel tips,' we'll need more casual clothes than anything else. Don't forget a bathing suit and thongs for the beach stops and the ship's swimming pool."

"We ought to wear lots of white outfits and our candle necklaces so passengers will know who we are," Jess suggested.

"Great idea," Melanie told her.

"We're going!" Tricia exclaimed. "We're really going! I'm beginning to believe it."

"Me too!" Melanie exclaimed. "We're going-going-going on a Caribbean cruise, and I'm so excited I could flip."

"Maybe we're all just dreaming together," Tricia remarked. "You know, a mass dream."

"I don't think so," Melanie replied.

"Tell us more about clothes," Cara said.

Melanie decided that Cara must be nervous about the cruise, too. "I think the thing to do is to get out a suitcase and see what seems right from our closets."

Becky wobbled her head crazily. "This summer's turned out so differently than we expected when we started the club. Tricia thought maybe she'd be visiting cousins in Virginia, and Jess's family was going to Hawaii. Instead, Jess and Melanie ended up in Israel—"

"And your mom got married!" Tricia put in.

"And now we're going to the Caribbean!" Jess added. "What a great summer!"

"We'd better get packing!" Cara told them.

They swung their legs over the benches and jumped up, every one of them talking at once.

"Tomorrow we'll be on the *Golden Isle*!" Melanie said, hurrying along with them.

Jess hopped on her bike and was the first to take off. "See you guys at the crack of dawn tomorrow morning!"

"At the crack of dawn!" Melanie answered.

Before long, they were all yelling, "See you!" and riding off down the driveway.

Melanie rushed for the side door of her house. *Can five twelve-year-old girls really take care of so many kids on a cruise ship?* she wondered again.

As if that weren't enough to worry about, brother William and sister Silvee would be two of the kids to take care of on the ship. William was the biggest problem, since he didn't listen to her, Melanie thought.

She wondered if the other kids would!

CHAPTER

2

Pink rays of sunlight pierced the morning darkness as Melanie and her family rode to the Los Angeles airport. From the backseat, Melanie watched Mom drive the white Buick, handling the steering wheel easily. Mom's black hair was done up in a twist poked through with ivory chopsticks.

Silvee sat in the front middle seat, the back of her little head scarcely showing over the seat.

Next came Auntie Ying-Ying by the passenger-seat window. In the dim morning light, her hair looked more gray than black.

Melanie sat between her ten-year-old brother, William, and Uncle Gwo-Jenn. Luckily William was dozing or dazing—either one being his best state of mind. Uncle Gwo-Jenn's eyelids were also "resting," as he called it, probably because he was older than Auntie Ying-Ying.

"Where's the cruise ship?" Silvee piped in her sweet five-year-old voice.

Mom darted a loving smile at Silvee. "First you go to the airport, then you'll fly to Atlanta and change planes there. Next, you fly to the island of Puerto Rico, and *then* you'll get on the cruise ship."

"Oh," Silvee answered, still puzzled.

Auntie Ying-Ying spoke gently. "Much to learn. Silvee have much yet to learn."

Uncle Gwo-Jenn just smiled.

He and Auntie were so different, it was amazing they got along. For one thing, they'd taken a cruise years ago and even though they'd had a good time, Uncle Gwo-Jenn thought one cruise was plenty for a lifetime. Still, he wanted to see Auntie off at the airport this morning.

Melanie strained her neck to look out the back window. She caught a glimpse of the Bennetts' maroon mini-van and was glad that the other TCCers were right behind them.

Beside her, William's eyes remained closed, his head resting back on the seat. "Don't worry," he muttered. "They're back there."

"How'd you even know I was looking?" Melanie asked. "Your eyes were closed—"

"I know everything . . . everything," her brother returned. "I see through my eyelids."

"Come *on*!"

Mom and Dad claimed ten-year-old brothers were often nuisances, but William was worse than a nuisance. He was an aggravation. Melanie suddenly thought, *What if there are lots of kids like him on the ship?*

"I see everything," William intoned. "I am William, superhuman being."

She checked her new pink cotton Tee, then smoothed

her white slacks. No sense arguing with him this morning. At least not about seeing through eyelids. It would be bad enough to be in charge of this "superhuman being"—and twenty-four others. She hoped they wouldn't all be super-human.

He pretended to be asleep even when they drove up at the airport unloading zone.

Mom eyed him in the mirror and called back, "William, you can wake up now and help with the suitcases."

Melanie watched her brother open the car door, his eyes still shut, then bump his head on the door frame as he got out. Climbing out behind him, she couldn't resist saying, "I guess you can't see upward through your eyelids."

He shouted a fierce "Hiii-ee-yah!" and karate chopped wildly at her.

She jumped back. "Stop it, William! Look, now people are staring at us!"

William bowed to the bystanders. "Honorable kung fu expert at your service," he explained. "Kung fu is honorable ancient Chinese martial art."

His "sidewalk audience" tried not to laugh, and Melanie wanted to karate chop him herself. She hissed, "You are em-barrassing . . . embarrassing to all of us!"

He grinned happily. "Glad to hear it."

"Please stop it, William," she begged. "Please be good on the trip."

"Chop, chop," he answered to be more embarrassing yet. "Chop, chop, I be good."

Melanie decided to ignore him since the rest of their family was already out on the sidewalk.

Mom must have noticed William's chop-chop talk because she warned, "William. . . !"

A "robot voice" announced from an overhead speaker, *"Cars in the loading zone must move on quickly. No parking is allowed in the loading zone. Unattended cars in the loading zone will be towed away. Cars in the loading zone must move on quickly. . . ."*

Yipes! Behind them, Uncle Gwo-Jenn kissed Auntie Ying-Ying's cheek, and her aunt kissed him, too. They were gray-haired grown-ups, and the sight of them kissing was almost as embarrassing as William's karate and chop-chop talk, Melanie thought.

She turned away quickly.

"Thank goodness, there's the Bennetts' mini-van pulling up there ahead of us." She hoped they hadn't noticed her embarrassing family.

Amazingly, William helped Uncle Gwo-Jenn get the luggage from the car trunk. Moments later, they lined up at the outside check-in, and Mom kissed each of them goodbye. "Are you sure you don't want me to stay with you until you board the plane?" she asked anxiously. "I can park in short-term—"

"We fine," Auntie Ying-Ying replied with firmness. "Parking hard here. I take good care of childrens."

Mom gave Auntie a hug. "Thank you, Ying-Ying."

Up ahead in the loading zone, Melanie was glad to see Mrs. Bennett give Tricia a kiss, because here came her own mom now. She was beautiful in her lavender crinkly cotton shorts and blouse outfit. She also wore her I-love-you-kids expression, which meant she'd kiss all of them—not that she'd make a big spectacle of it.

Melanie waited to see how her sister and her brother—

especially her brother—responded. First, Silvee gave Mom a big hug and kissed her in return. William barely allowed Mom to kiss his cheek as he muttered, "Mush!"

"Oh, William," Mom said, disappointed. "Don't forget, your father and I expect you to behave yourself."

To make up for him, Melanie gave Mom a big hug and kiss. Going away on this trip, it felt comforting for her mother to hold her for a moment. "Don't worry, I'll try to do a good job. I'll do my very best—"

"You have a good time," Mom answered. "I know you'll do a terrific job with the kids' program, so don't worry. You do a great job at everything you undertake. You're supposed to have a fun time on the cruise, too."

"I'll try," Melanie promised.

She smiled at herself. Probably her modeling jobs in New York had made her too worried about doing a good job. Dad said being too responsible was also typical for an oldest child in a family. But she couldn't help thinking that Santa Rosita Travel had arranged the free cruise for the TCCers to work, not just to have fun. Besides, Santa Rosita Travel was also buying their shore excursion tickets, which were very expensive.

Uncle Gwo-Jenn waved a last goodbye, then headed for the Buick's front seat. "Have a great time!" he called back.

"We'll try!" Melanie responded.

Auntie Ying-Ying waved another goodbye at him, then turned to survey their luggage. "Make sure all red cruise-line tags tied on suitcase handles and no luggage missing." She told Melanie as if she couldn't read, "Red tag means suitcases go straight to *Golden Isle* ship. Good idea, huh?"

"Good idea," Melanie agreed.

She thought that her aunt might be eccentric or funny or peculiar—whatever—but Dad often said that Auntie Ying-Ying had an organized way of handling matters. In fact, he joked that she'd make a good army general.

"All suitcases ready," her aunt announced. She turned to Melanie. "I sit between Silvee and William, so you be with TCC girls on airplane."

Melanie gave her a heartfelt "Thanks, Auntie!"

She turned to Mom's white Buick and waved again as they drove off. Probably Mom felt confident about Auntie Ying-Ying being in charge since Mrs. Wong would be on the trip, too. Mom knew the travel agent from church.

People lined up behind them, and before long the other TCCers stood in line. Last night on the phone, they'd all decided to wear Tees and cotton pants for the flight to Puerto Rico, so they wouldn't freeze in the plane's air-conditioning. Tricia's outfit was a seafoam green color. Jess wore a no-nonsense tan two-piece. Cara, a peach Tee and darker peach pants. Becky wore all blue, which looked great with her blue eyes. And they all wore their TCC necklaces, which were small brass candle-shaped pendants hanging from white ribbons.

"Ready?" Jess called up the line to Melanie.

"Ready as I'll ever be!"

Auntie Ying-Ying had waved Mrs. Bennett on. "I watch girls for you, don't worry!"

Just then a police car drove along in the airport traffic, and Mrs. Bennett yelled, "Thanks! I'd better get moving!"

"Bye, Mom!" Tricia called out.

"Thanks for driving us here, Mrs. Bennett!" the others yelled.

Melanie was about to turn toward the uniformed airline man checking them in when she noticed Tricia begin to whisper to Jess, Cara, and Becky. The next moment, they turned around carefully to glance at someone joining the line behind them. Melanie looked with them.

A boy, about six . . . and a girl, about ten. Just behind them stood a grandparent-type couple.

Melanie saw the TCCers turn away from them in shock, and she looked away herself. What was that about?

She was vaguely aware of her aunt checking in their luggage and warning the airline man not to lose it.

Just then, Tricia ambled up to Melanie and murmured, "Don't look now, but those kids who just got in line a few people behind us are Karla and Jason Hermann. I baby-sat them one time."

"Who?" Melanie asked. She'd never seen the kids or the grandmotherly woman before, although the overweight grandfatherly type with the sunglasses looked familiar.

Tricia drew a breath. "Their mother is Mrs. Hermann, the very Mrs. Hermann who tried to help Mrs. Leffler kidnap me at the mall. You know, about the drug-money laundering."

Melanie felt her mouth drop open. "That . . . older man is the one we saw once at Leffler's Fine Chocolates! His sunglasses threw me!"

"It's Sid Hermann, for sure," Tricia answered.

Still stunned, Melanie managed, "But I thought he was in jail with his son and the others."

"Believe me, I did, too," Tricia answered. "Yipes! I just noticed. They've got the very same red cruise-line tickets on their luggage! I can't believe this!"

Melanie darted an innocent glance down the line of passengers. Sure enough, the Hermann luggage handles held the same red cruise-line name tags as theirs! "Why would they be going on a Caribbean cruise?"

Tricia shrugged unhappily. "I just hope we don't have to baby-sit those kids."

Goosebumps raced up Melanie's neck. "I hope we don't have to, either!"

Seeing the Hermanns in line outside at the airline check-in was bad enough, but then they appeared inside at the boarding gate. Mrs. Wong stood in the Gate 8 area holding up a red *"Golden Isle"* sign. The cruise passengers gathered around her for instructions.

"We'll wait over here on these chairs," Melanie told Auntie Ying-Ying. Then she whispered to the TCCers, "Let's stay as far away from the Hermanns as possible."

"Good idea," Becky whispered back.

"Sitting down is good idea," Auntie Ying-Ying said as she sunk onto a boarding area chair. "Feet tired. But, no worry, feet fine on cruise ship."

Melanie darted a glance at William, who was pretending to karate chop one of the nearby kids. She rolled her eyes at the TCCers.

"It's okay, Melanie," Jess said. "Believe me, I understand. My brothers don't karate chop, but they do plenty of other dumb stuff."

Auntie Ying-Ying ordered, "William, come sit by your auntie."

He frowned. "Why?"

"Sit, William," their aunt answered. "Sit."

He sat.

One thing about her aunt, when she ordered William to behave, he did it, Melanie thought. She'd have to try her aunt's "Sit!" command on him.

She eyed the Hermanns, who sat near the boarding-gate windows. They looked out the windows at their plane as if they hadn't recognized them.

"Safe, so far," she whispered to Tricia. "Maybe they're still half-asleep."

"Let's sit with our backs to them," Cara suggested.

But when they boarded the plane, it was more difficult. They found the Hermanns settled in the first-class section of the plane as if they owned it—grandparents in front, and Karla and Jason in the seats behind them.

Melanie passed them quickly, glad that Mr. Hermann didn't seem to recognize her. She pretended not to know him or the kids. Then behind her, she heard Tricia say, "Well, hi, Karla and Jason! Fancy seeing you here!"

"Hi, Tricia!" Jason answered excitedly, as if he were pleased to see her.

Karla didn't sound quite as pleased, but managed a cool "Hello. I thought I saw you."

"Small world, isn't it?" Tricia asked.

Thankfully, no one replied.

When Melanie arrived in coach class with the others, she felt like fainting. "How could you be relaxed?" she asked Tricia. "How could you do it?"

Tricia raised her shoulders. "I don't know myself. Only that it helps sometimes if you know acting."

"I guess it must," Melanie answered.

She understood what Tricia meant. Tricia often acted in church or community plays. Melanie decided that acting, like modeling, had to help with confidence.

"Besides," Tricia added, "I felt as if God was giving me peace in spite of them."

Melanie shook her head. "Whatever, it was surprising."

She waited in the aisle while other people sat down, and tried to keep her mind on their seating arrangement. The TCCers had seats in a row: Cara by the window, Jess in the middle, Tricia on the aisle.

Melanie saw hers was on the opposite side of the aisle with Becky beside her in the middle section. Next to Becky in the mid-section, Auntie Ying-Ying, Silvee, and William were already seated.

Melanie felt surprised that Becky chose to sit with her. Becky and Tricia were best friends—and they definitely had not been fighting. Maybe Becky understood what it felt like to be a newcomer since she'd just moved to her new step-father's house and would start at a different school soon. Whatever the cause, it felt good for Becky to sit with her.

At last everyone in the row was seated. Melanie stuck her big leather model's bag under the seat in front of her, then sat down herself. She noticed her aunt clasped her new video camera on her lap.

Once they were seated, Melanie whispered to Becky, "What are we going to do about the Hermanns on the ship?"

Becky looked as nervous about it as Melanie felt. "I don't know. Maybe Tricia has an idea. I still can't believe they'd be going on this trip. It feels like a nightmare."

Melanie nodded and fastened her seat belt. When she

looked up, she noticed streams of kids coming down the aisle: the boy William had karate chopped . . . another one who'd raced around with him. It looked like fifty kids, but maybe most wouldn't be on the cruise ship.

Melanie leaned over the aisle and whispered to Tricia, "Becky and I want to know, what if we have to take care of those Hermann kids on the ship?"

"I guess we'll just have to see what happens," Tricia whispered back.

"How do you think the grandfather got out of jail?"

Tricia shrugged. "The FBI man, Mr. Smith, said they didn't have as much evidence on him as they did on his son or the others. Probably his lawyers got him out for . . . you know, lack of evidence. Not enough proof on him."

"Maybe they don't have the exact same red cruise tags as we do," Melanie said.

"That's what I hoped, but Jess sneaked by them while you went into the airport. They're the very same cruise-line tags as ours. *Golden Cruises.*"

Becky had leaned over to listen. "Maybe they're going on a different ship that belongs to the same cruise line."

"Yeah, maybe that's it," Melanie put in hopefully.

"We'll just have to see if the Hermanns end up on our ship, that's all," Becky said. "If so, we'll have to trust the Lord to help us."

"I guess so," Tricia answered.

Melanie sat back since a flight attendant was beginning to give the safety information. Pressing her head against the seat, she said, "I can't believe this could happen. . . ."

Beside her, Becky put in, "Me, neither. I can't believe we're really going."

For an instant, Melanie wondered about telling Auntie Ying-Ying about the Hermanns. But considering how excited her aunt got about things, it was probably better not to tell her.

Once the plane was up in the air, a flight attendant pulled the curtain between first class and coach.

"Thank goodness," Becky said.

"Anything to separate us from them," Melanie agreed. "Even a curtain helps."

She reached down for her leather bag and pulled out the cruise brochure. She'd treat this job just like a modeling assignment; she'd learn everything she could in advance. Glancing at the white cruise ship on the cover, she hoped everything would turn out as fun as it looked.

After a time, the mingled smells of coffee and bacon drifted through the plane's cabin. The pilot began to tell about the sights below: mountains, desert, and a huge lake. Melanie stood in the aisle to look out the other TCCers' window.

"Isn't it wonderful?" she said. "I love flying."

Jess replied, "It's just a good thing this flight won't be as long as the one we took to Israel."

"You're right about that," Melanie agreed. This trip *only* crossed the United States, then flew a short distance down to the island of Puerto Rico. She returned to her seat and checked out the flight in the back of the airline magazine. Yep, the trip was as long as she'd thought.

After a while, the flight attendants served a breakfast of fresh orange juice, cheesy omelets with bits of parsley and bright red cherry tomatoes, hot buttered English muffins, and curls of crisp bacon.

Melanie sat back to enjoy every bite, since last night she'd been too excited to eat much dinner.

"Nice, huh?" Auntie Ying-Ying asked across Becky. "One week, no cooking, no shopping, no washing dishes."

"Nice, all right," Melanie agreed.

Over breakfast, she and Becky discussed the summer, then school next month and school clothing. Before long, their trays were removed, and she thumbed through the shopping catalog. Next, a movie was shown on the small screen. A violent murder-mystery film.

"No look," Auntie Ying-Ying warned them. "Too bad for you." She had Silvee busy with a coloring book and William playing a new Game Boy video game.

William darted a glance at Melanie, then smirked in his usual superior way.

"Too bad for you," he mimicked nastily.

Melanie glanced up at the movie herself. A car crash had just taken place.

She remarked to Becky, "I wonder if the actors ever think about God."

Becky shrugged. "Probably some do."

"Probably they don't!" William shot over at them.

"Ignore him," Melanie said.

Becky smiled and nodded, most likely because she had a younger brother herself.

Except for William and the Hermanns sitting up in first class, everything was perfect, Melanie thought. Finally she remembered to pray.

Lord, please let everything be perfect. And if it can't be totally perfect, please let it be . . . ummm . . . exciting. Yes, exciting!

She hesitated.

But help me to be calm in the middle of any excitement.

CHAPTER

3

When Melanie and the others made their way off the plane, the first-class passengers were already gone.

"No Hermanns," Jess whispered back to her.

Melanie nodded, relieved, then repeated it back to Becky. "No Hermanns."

Becky let out a deep breath. "Thank goodness!"

"That's what I say," Melanie replied.

They hadn't seen the Hermanns since they'd boarded the plane in Los Angeles—nor when they raced to change planes in Atlanta, nor on the plane from Atlanta to Puerto Rico. On the last flight, they couldn't see into the first-class section, since it was to the left of the plane's boarding door. After that, the flight to San Juan, Puerto Rico, had been so interesting Melanie had nearly forgotten about them.

As the plane had descended through fluffy white clouds, they'd seen the big green island in the midst of the sea. The blue Atlantic Ocean rolled along one side of Puerto Rico, and the turquoise Caribbean Sea on the other. When they flew lower, even the old walls of a huge fortress had come into view.

Now, in the airport, a short young woman with a great tan and long, wavy dark hair held a *Golden Isle* sign. The name tag pinned to her navy blue suit jacket spelled out *Steffi*. She beamed at them. "*Golden Isle?*"

"That's us!" Melanie chorused with the others.

"Welcome to Puerto Rico!" Steffi exclaimed. She was as short as Jess and spoke with a slight foreign accent. Italian maybe. Whatever, she looked way too young for the squinting lines on her forehead.

"Thanks," Melanie answered with the others.

Steffi seemed stressed, but she still had a sweet smile. Suddenly her brown eyes widened. "Hey! Are you the girls helping with the youth program?"

"Yep," Jess answered. "We're the Twelve Candles Club."

Steffi let out a breath of relief. "Oh boy, I'm glad for your help! Otherwise, I'd have to take care of all the kids in my spare time and, let me tell you, when you work on a ship, you're very busy."

She looked so glad to see them that Melanie wondered, *How bad can the kids in a youth program be?*

Steffi stood on tiptoe with her sign and called out, "I'll meet everyone by the baggage claim area, then we take buses to the ship. Watch for *Golden Isle* signs when you have your suitcases. We'll take care of you from here on, so relax and have a good time. Meet you at baggage claim."

Probably she's repeated those words over and over to thousands of tourists, Melanie thought.

"Thank you, Steffi, thank you!" Auntie Ying-Ying told her, then swept along with the TCCers. "Very good news. Nothing to worry about. They take care of us now. Only good time ahead. We follow signs to baggage."

Melanie glanced around nearby rows of seats, then up and down the center aisle. She side-mouthed to Cara, "Phew! No Hermanns here, either."

Cara nodded, and they all set off through the small airport for the baggage area.

"Seems like they just disappeared," Jess said.

An electric cart beeped behind them, making them jump out of the way.

Tricia remarked, "They're probably the type who'd take an electric cart so they wouldn't have to walk."

"Hey, there's an idea," Melanie answered. She turned to her aunt. "Want to ride in a cart instead of walking?"

Auntie Ying-Ying shook her head. "No way! No way! Better walk so no get fatter. We eat much on cruise ship."

Melanie nodded. It was best to agree with Auntie Ying-Ying to avoid long discussions.

"What if we all get fat?" Becky asked.

"Don't even mention it," Melanie answered. "It'd be the end of what's left of my modeling career."

Auntie Ying-Ying laughed. "You girls skinny like bean strings. Very skinny bean strings."

Laughing, they made their way with the crowd, following the overhead baggage claim signs. It was exciting to be at the San Juan Airport in the midst of scurrying travelers.

"We buy candy bars at newspaper shop," Auntie Ying-Ying told them. "It always takes much time for suitcases to come off airplane. Much time."

Jess howled, "And get fatter on candy bars!"

Auntie Ying-Ying slapped a hand to her lips to hide her own laughter. "Is okay one time. One candy bar only."

Melanie had to smile. The TCCers liked her aunt, and Silvee—even William. Best of all, her aunt was keeping a firm grip on both of them.

It did feel as if they were on a vacation, Melanie thought as everyone bought candy bars, then later as she and the TCCers strolled out. She bit into her side of a Snickers bar she was sharing with Silvee.

In the baggage claim area, there was no sign of the Hermanns, either. Melanie turned to Jess, since her father was an airline pilot. "Where could the Hermanns be? With those red tags on their suitcases, they have to be here."

Jess shrugged. "I suppose they could have someone pick up their luggage and take it to the ship."

"Like who?" Becky asked.

Cara glanced out the glass doors. "Maybe a limo driver, like those limos lined up out there."

"Could be," Tricia said, eyeing the limos. "Karla and Jason's parents sure live expensively from what I saw of their house."

"On the other hand," Jess put in, "maybe they got off the plane in Atlanta."

"Let's hope that's it," Melanie said. "But they did have red cruise tags like ours on their suitcases."

Auntie Ying-Ying asked, "Who you girls talk about?"

"Some people we saw on the plane," Melanie answered, determined not to go into too much detail. "Tricia baby-sat the kids once." Her aunt would worry herself crazy if she knew the Hermanns were connected with drug money. Besides, since Sid Hermann wasn't in jail—maybe he was innocent.

Auntie Ying-Ying shook her head with amazement. "You girls know everybody in Santa Rosita, don't you? Everybody!"

Tricia gave a laugh. "Not quite everybody, but we know a lot of interesting people."

"Is good," Auntie said, keeping her eye on the luggage turntable. "Is good to know lots of people."

Becky pointed over the crowd. "There's Steffi with the *Golden Isle* sign."

Sure enough, the tour guide stood just outside the baggage claim area. Melanie glanced at the turntable again. "And here come our suitcases!" she exclaimed, heading for them. As she grabbed hers, her heart leapt again with excitement. "Whoa, our suitcases are here . . . and we're here . . . and we're really going on a cruise ship!"

Before long, they'd pulled their suitcases from the turntable and joined Steffi. "Straight ahead out those doors," she told them. "There'll be a guide to put you on a bus to the ship. Stay with your group and watch for *Golden Isle* signs."

They piled their suitcases onto a cart, then pushed them outside into the bright sunshine. More friendly guides with signs directed them to a row of buses. "To the first bus, please. *Golden Isle* passengers to the first bus. Your driver will put your luggage in the bus compartment."

Passengers milled about, making sure the bus driver put their bags in the luggage compartment, and Melanie decided to keep an eye on her blue suitcase, too. Everything was going along fine except for one thing.

"Look," she said, her stomach turning over uneasily. "Look at all of those Santa Rosita kids! How can we ever take care of that many of them?!"

During the bus ride to the ship, there were glimpses of San Juan: cobblestone streets, old white-painted churches, balconies enclosed with black wrought iron. Soon they drove along the shoreline and someone called out, "There she is! That's the *Golden Isle*!"

Melanie joined the others peering out the bus windows. An enormous white ship rose before them. "It's beautiful!" she exclaimed. "Even more beautiful than in the pictures!"

Minutes later, she was on the dock near the huge white ship, her hair blowing in the balmy breeze. Her heart thumped to the beat of the music that spilled from a lower deck.

"Calypso music," Tricia explained.

"I don't know much about music," Melanie admitted.

"It's West Indian music with some jazz to it," Becky put in. "Remember when we worked at the Brazilian jazz party at the LeRoy estate?"

Melanie shook her head. "I wasn't in the club yet."

"Oops, I forgot," Becky answered. "Sorry."

Once in a while, Melanie didn't feel entirely part of the club yet. They'd started the club in June, and she'd been invited to join later. She hoped she wouldn't spoil things for them, she thought as they started up the ship's gangway.

The *Golden Isle* was enormous, all right, its bow rising gracefully in a sharp curve to the layers of open decks above. "I feel like we're in that cruise ship brochure!" She was glad to see that her friends seemed just as excited. "I can't believe we're here!"

"We are," Auntie Ying-Ying said from in front of her. "It is happening to you, Melanie Lin."

The security area resembled those at airports, Melanie thought. She followed other passengers in a line, then placed her hand luggage on a conveyer belt table so an inspector could see into it through an X-ray. Next, she walked through a metal detector and was glad her brass candle-shaped pendant didn't set it off.

Behind her, William asked the inspector loudly, "Do you expect bad guys to get on the ship?"

"William!" Melanie hissed at him.

The inspector answered, "We just want all of you to be safe. Now, if you'll step aside, please—"

While they waited for Auntie Ying-Ying to come through, Melanie whispered to Tricia, "What was it your FBI man said about smuggling drugs to the Caribbean?"

Tricia shook her head. "Smuggling drugs *through* the Caribbean, not *to* the Caribbean. Don't mention it! Our trouble with those drug money laundering guys was bad enough!"

After they'd passed through security, *Golden Isle* guides directed them through a check-in area near the ship.

The woman at the table beamed. "Here's your information packet, which includes a map of the ship, ports of call material, and your cabin keys. Welcome to the *Golden Isle!*"

Melanie felt like dancing with Auntie Ying-Ying but settled for an excited, "We're going! We're really going!"

"Big deal," William muttered, and Silvee jumped up and down with excitement.

"Come on," Melanie said, "let's head out!"

The other TCCers had their information packets, too, and they all headed for the line of passengers climbing up the gangway steps.

Once there, the line moved quickly. When it did stop, Melanie bounced to the rhythms of the calypso music, holding on to the railing and her model's bag.

"It seems like a dream, doesn't it?" Becky asked from behind her.

Melanie nodded. "It does! Let's face it, this is no place to do our klutz act."

"You know it," Jess answered, her hazel eyes taking in the scene around them. "But we're really here!"

Melanie might not have been a TCC member long, but she knew what the "klutz act" was. It meant crossing their eyes, walking knock-kneed, and calling out, "Klutz-klutz-klutz!" to make fun of themselves for being so klutzy.

"I've been feeling bad about klutzing anyhow," Becky said. "Gram says there are people who are really cross-eyed or knock-kneed, and it might seem as if we were making fun of them instead of ourselves. Maybe we'd better not do it anymore."

Melanie raised her brows. "I never thought of it like that. Well, who needs to show off being klutzy anyhow?"

Tricia laughed. "Anyone can see we are without trying!"

Everyone else laughed as they agreed and walked up the gangway steps. Up close, the ship's paint was a blinding white, but bumpy, as if it had been chipped and painted often.

When they reached the top of the gangway, rows of white-jacketed attendants stood like honor guards, their black slacks sharply creased and black shoes shining. The row of passengers moved forward. Suddenly an attendant stepped toward Melanie, a white-gloved hand outstretched for her key and model's bag. His name tag spelled out *Ramone*.

"Welcome aboard," Ramone said with a foreign accent. "May I show you to your suite on the Royale Deck?"

She felt uncertain, but ahead of them, Auntie Ying-Ying waited with Silvee and William and their attendants. "Come on, Melanie," her aunt urged. "Come on."

Melanie gave Ramone the key and her model's bag, then stepped into the ship and caught her breath. A huge chandelier hung overhead, velvety red carpeting lay underfoot, and plush furnishings turned the entry into a floating palace. Everywhere, attendants ushered in new passengers.

Other passengers studied maps of the ship as they found their way around. Melanie glanced back and saw the other TCCers coming aboard, as wide-eyed as she felt.

She overheard a steward remark, "Our last plane load's coming in, a family coming by limo. Almost ready to sail."

A family coming by limo. . . ?

Melanie swallowed and hoped it wasn't who she thought it might be. Before she could worry about it, she spied Steffi standing with other navy blue uniformed staff members.

"Hi, TCCers!" Steffi called out to them. "Stop for just a minute. I want you to meet our cruise director, Maxwell Thornton. Maxwell, these are the girls for the special youth program. Girls, this is our boss."

Maxwell Thornton was tall, not quite handsome, and

wore a white nautical officer's hat over his brown hair. He gave them a wide smile, which looked great with his dark tan. "Welcome aboard the *Golden Isle*, girls," he said, making them sound like five-year-olds. "We're *so* glad to have you as part of the crew."

"What do you do?" Jess asked him.

"I'm an *important* person on the ship," Maxwell answered. *"Very important."*

Steffi bit her lips, but her eyes filled with laughter. Finally she managed, "See you, girls! We can't hold up boarding, even if our cruise director is *very important.*"

Maxwell called behind them, "Be sure to come to the 'Welcome Aboard Talk' I give in the Ruby Lounge later."

"We will!" Melanie answered and moved on.

It sounded like Mr. Cruise Director, Maxwell Thornton, was an out-and-out bragger. She hoped he wasn't going to be difficult, too. She hurried along behind her attendant through a maze of hallways.

Before long, they caught up with her aunt, Silvee, and William. The other TCCers and their attendants came right behind them down a hallway that Ramone called a "corridor."

"We're here!" Jess announced, dancing in place. "We're here!" She whispered so Ramone wouldn't hear, "Hey, what about that stuck-up cruise director?"

Tricia laughed. "Definitely a case of *very important*. We might have to be careful of him."

Melanie guessed that the other TCCers hadn't heard the remark about a family coming by limo, and decided there was no need to mention it now. She just hoped it wasn't the Hermanns.

Ramone stopped. "Your suite, Royale Deck, number 300."

"Easy for remember," Auntie Ying-Ying remarked. "Royale 300. Blue carpet. Different decks have different carpet?" she asked Ramone.

"Yes, to help know where you are," he replied. "Royale Deck has blue carpet, Ruby Deck has red, Emerald Deck has green. . . ."

Melanie noticed the other TCCers were next door in 302, and their travel agent, Mrs. Wong, was being escorted to 304. Probably their whole group was close together. So far, everything seemed perfect.

Inside, their cabin had cream walls and blue carpeting. The cabin was actually two small rooms somewhat separated by thin brass trellising. Straight ahead was a small white, tan, and blue bathroom. To the left, a blue fold-out couch stood under the square window. Two twin beds lined the walls on the other end of the room. A chest of drawers topped by a large mirror stood on the far wall between the two twin beds.

"This is it?" William asked, disappointed.

"This it," Auntie Ying-Ying answered. "And 'suite' means is bigger than regular cabin. Don't worry, William. We here mainly to sleep and change clothes. Plenty places on ship . . . game rooms, youth rooms, swimming pools, many decks, library . . . many places when we not off to visit islands."

William still looked skeptical, but he said, "Good."

Silvee beamed. "It's nice and cozy. I love it! I love it! I like sleeping close to all of you."

Melanie had mixed feelings about sharing the small suite

with her aunt and William for a week but decided to keep her mouth shut for a change.

"William and I sleep in twin beds," Auntie Ying-Ying decided. "Silvee and Melanie sleep on fold-out couch."

"Yea, Melanie!" Silvee called out with delight.

Glad for her little sister's love, Melanie gave her a hug. Auntie smiled. "We unpack hand luggage now. Suitcases be delivered after dinner."

It didn't take Melanie long to unpack her bag: wallet, hairbrush, nightie, thongs . . . a change of clothes in case her suitcase was delayed. She hung her clothes in a narrow locker-like closet. She hadn't brought much money, so her wallet went into the built-in chest's locking drawer, as did William's and Silvee's.

"There," Melanie said, "all set for now. May I go next door to the TCCers' cabin . . . or is it a suite?"

"All here on Royale Deck have suite," her aunt answered, "but everybody say 'cabin.' Now, first thing to do on cruise ship is have bon voyage party on decks for sailing. Next comes lifeboat drill."

"Lifeboat drill?" Melanie asked.

"Lifeboat drill?" William echoed.

Auntie Ying-Ying nodded. "Just like an airplane, flight attendant tell safety rules. Only on ship, first thing when sailing, they give everybody lifeboat drill."

"Right away?" William asked.

"Best time to practice," their aunt replied. "Better than far out at sea if ship have trouble."

"ALL PASSENGERS ABANDON SHIP!" William announced in a fakey low voice. "ALL PASSENGERS ABANDON SHIP!" He made a low foghorn sound,

"OOO-AAA-OOO-AAA-OOO!"

"Stop it!" Melanie yelled.

"William!" Auntie Ying-Ying warned.

Silvee's brown eyes widened with fear. "You mean . . . we might drown. . . ?"

"No," Auntie answered firmly. "That why we have lifeboat drill. If trouble, we put on life vests and go straight to Lifeboat 30, then we all go together."

William joked, "So we all die together—"

"William!" Auntie warned, "think before speak!"

She turned to Silvee, who looked more fearful yet. "We not die. We go together on small boat until rescue boat comes, or maybe even to island. Robinson Crusoe Island, like at Disneyland. That was much fun, huh?"

Silvee nodded, not looking quite as fearful.

"We'll be all right, Silvee," Melanie assured her, though she was unsure herself.

William's brown eyes twinkled with more mischief, and Melanie shot him a warning glance. She hoped he wouldn't be trouble on this trip.

Auntie Ying-Ying showed them the orange life vests in the top of each closet. "Says here how to put on," she said, pointing out tags with writing on the vests. Remember lifeboat station number for us. See, marked on wall. Lifeboat Station 30, almost like Suite 300. Easy to remember."

"Okay, I've got it," Melanie said, tired of the worrisome subject. William would probably keep at it, too. "May I go over to the TCCers' cabin until we sail?"

"Sure," her aunt answered. "Take key. I have other key. I take Silvee and William to deck for sailing party. Sailing soon! Don't miss sailing. Is beautiful sight from deck."

"I won't miss it."

As Melanie stepped out into the corridor, she glanced about, half expecting to see the Hermanns. If they'd signed up with Santa Rosita Travel, they'd probably be in a nearby cabin, too.

No sign of them.

She pounded out a knock-knock-knockety-knock on the door of Cabin 302.

Tricia swung open the door.

"Ready for the sailing party?" Melanie asked.

"Ready to go!" Tricia answered. "TCCers, gather up your keys. Are we ready for the great sailing adventure to begin?"

"Yes!" they all chorused.

Me too! Melanie thought. She felt ready for the adventure to begin!

CHAPTER

4

Melanie and the other TCCers stood on the Royale Deck and watched the sailors wind in the huge mooring lines. A calypso band played down on the dock, and people waved up at friends on the ship, calling out, "Bon voyage! Bon voyage!"

Steffi rushed over to join the TCCers, beaming and carrying a huge paper bag. "May I watch with you girls?"

"Sure," they answered.

"We're honored," Cara said, who was in to vocabulary building lately.

As if to explain joining them, Steffi said, "It's my guess that you girls are more fun than most of the passengers."

Melanie gave a laugh. "Come *on*!"

"It's the truth," Steffi assured her. "Let's face it, not all passengers are fun. I guess I still have a lot of girl in me, that's why I'm glad you're here."

"Glad to hear it," Jess replied. "Actually, you seem pretty young yourself."

"You do," Melanie agreed. Steffi looked about nineteen except for the squint lines in her forehead.

"Thanks!" Steffi answered with a laugh. "You know, I've worked on cruise ships for four years, but it's still fun for me to watch arrivals and departures. If the excitement ever stops, I think it'll be time for me to find a new career."

When they all glanced back down to the cargo deck, Melanie's eyes stopped on two large wooden boxes. "What are those wooden boxes down there?" The boxes looked like inexpensive coffins!

As Steffi looked down, two crewmen began to carry one of them into the ship.

Steffi answered with reluctance. "I'm sorry you saw them. They're actually empty coffins."

"Coffins!" Becky exclaimed.

"Shhh!" Steffi told her. "There's no sense in worrying passengers about them."

Melanie whispered, "Do people die on cruise ships?"

Steffi nodded unhappily. "You guessed it. Just look around at all of the elderly passengers. If it happens to be their time to die, they could die at home or in a hospital or on a cruise ship, couldn't they? No one knows when it'll happen."

Melanie glanced at the passengers on their deck. Plenty of old people, no question about that. And it was true, people didn't know when they might die.

"A cruise is great for older people," Steffi told them. "For one thing, there's a doctor aboard almost all ships, and there're plenty of activities. Passengers can go on the land tours or just sit out on deck and enjoy the scenery. On board, there're movies, bingo, talent shows . . . lots of entertainment. Let's put it this way. Would you rather die in a hospital or on a cruise ship?"

"My dad's a doctor," Melanie remarked. "His hospitals in New York and Santa Rosita are as nice as hospitals can be, but I think it'd be a lot better to die on a cruise ship."

Steffi laughed. "With a chocolate eclair in your mouth."

"Yep," Melanie answered, "or a chocolate brownie."

Everyone agreed, laughing uncomfortably.

When Melanie glanced down to the cargo deck again, she remarked, "The coffins are gone."

"They're usually the last cargo loaded, so they can be unloaded fast," Steffi explained. "Let's not talk about it anymore, okay? We don't want to ruin anyone's trip."

"Good idea," Melanie decided. "And whatever we do, we don't want my aunt to hear about it. She'd . . . well, who knows what she'd say?"

"It's a deal," Steffi said. "Now, one reason I was looking for you girls is that after dinner, try to get right over to the youth rooms on your deck. Cabins 315 and 317. Have you seen them?"

"No," Melanie replied with the others. "I guess they must be on the other side of the stairway and elevators."

"Yep," Steffi said. "Even numbers on the port side of the ship, which means on the left-hand side if you're facing forward. Odd numbers on the starboard side, which means right-hand side."

"We'll check them out as soon as we can," Becky promised.

"No hurry," Steffi assured them. "But we'll need all of

you there in the youth rooms after dinner."

"We'll be there," Jess promised.

The calypso band on the dock played on, and the boat's horn gave a long, low blast.

Steffi opened her paper bag and flung colorful curls of confetti into the air over the TCCers. "Bon voyage!" she called out merrily. At the girls' questioning look, she threw more confetti. "It's French for 'Have a great cruise!' " She shouted another "Bon voyage!"

"Bon voyage!" Melanie echoed the passengers' excited cheering. Laughing and pulling a yellow curl of confetti from her hair, she threw it at Jess.

"Bon voyage!" the other TCCers echoed, throwing confetti, too. Soon everyone was throwing it.

The ship's band began to play calypso music with the band on the dock as the *Golden Isle* edged away from the dock. Slowly, the stately ship made its way from the harbor.

A waiter carrying a tray with drinks offered, "Would you girls care for Cokes?"

"Sure," Melanie replied. "Thanks."

His brown eyes twinkled, and the pink confetti hanging over his white-uniformed arm added to the festivities.

Another waiter followed with a tray of tiny sandwiches, and Melanie took three, realizing she was starved.

When she looked back, the docks at San Juan, Puerto Rico, were already receding behind them. They grew smaller and smaller in the distance until they disappeared from view, and the *Golden Isle* sailed alone in the inky blue sea. With the late-day sunshine sparkling on the water, it was a beautiful sight.

Once the ship was well under way, overhead speakers

crackled. *"We will be having a lifeboat drill shortly. All passengers are required by International Navigational Law to participate in the lifeboat drill. Please proceed to your cabins now and wait for further instructions. The crew will help anyone who needs assistance."*

Melanie didn't like the idea of a lifeboat drill, but she headed inside with the TCCers, who felt equally anxious about it. It would be far more pleasant to ignore the dangers of being at sea. Luckily, their cabins were nearby.

Giving her friends a wave, she called out, "See you."

She let herself into Cabin 300.

Silvee, William, and Auntie Ying-Ying were already there, pulling the orange vests from the top shelves of the narrow closets.

William called out, "ALL PASSENGERS ABANDON SHIP! ALL PASSENGERS ABANDON SHIP!"

Melanie rolled her eyes at him. It was bad enough to have seen the ship's coffins, and now to have the lifeboat drill with his "abandon ship" stuff—

"Enough, William!" Auntie Ying-Ying ordered. "Lifeboat drill is serious business. Very serious business."

Melanie helped Silvee put on her life vest, then tie it like the instructions on it showed. She grabbed her own orange vest from the closet shelf and looped up the ties to avoid tripping over them as she headed for the door. "If it's all right, I'll be next door with the TCCers—"

"All right, but remember Lifeboat 30 on Golden Deck," Auntie Ying-Ying answered. "Keep number in your head, Melanie. Golden Deck is two decks up. Here, take ship map so you don't get lost."

Melanie took the map. "Lifeboat 30, Golden Deck,"

Melanie repeated on her way out the door. She didn't want Silvee or William to know how uneasy she felt about the drill. Silvee would be scared, and William would never stop teasing. As for getting lost on the huge *Golden Isle*, it was possible.

She closed her cabin door and looked down the corridor. A family wearing orange life vests already headed the other way. For an instant, she fought the reality of the other sight down the corridor and then couldn't deny it.

Jason and Karla . . . and the older Hermanns!

They *were* on the ship!

Luckily they didn't look back. It occurred to her that Sid Hermann might recognize her from the time the TCCers had returned the $7,000 bank deposit to Leffler's Fine Chocolates, or from the newspaper pictures about it.

Clutching her "map of the ship," Melanie knocked on the TCCers' door.

Cara opened it. "It's Melanie—"

Melanie ducked in. "Close the door fast!"

Wide-eyed, Cara shut the door. "What's wrong? You look like you saw a ghost out there."

Melanie leaned against the cabin door and drew a calming breath. "Almost as bad . . . or maybe worse."

Jess, Becky, and Tricia stopped in the act of putting on their life vests. "What's wrong?"

"The Hermanns are staying in a cabin on this very corridor!" Melanie told them.

Tricia's green eyes bulged. "You're kidding!"

"I just saw them, but they didn't see me."

Tricia put a hand to her mouth. "I hoped their being on the plane was, you know . . . a coincidence."

"I wish I *were* kidding," Melanie said. "They're five doors away. It must be cabin 312." A new thought hit. "Maybe they bought discount tickets from Santa Rosita Travel, too."

For a change, Jess looked shaken. "But why would they go on the trip as soon as he gets out of jail?"

"Who knows?" Melanie answered.

"A cruise is supposed to be a great getaway trip for most people," Becky remarked.

Tricia had turned quiet, but now she said, "Maybe it's not a 'getaway' trip for the Hermanns."

"What do you mean?" Melanie asked.

"Drugs . . ." Tricia replied uneasily. "I told you what Mr. Thomas, the FBI man, said. Lots of drugs come into our country by way of Mexico and the Caribbean Islands."

Jess asked, "Do you think they plan to smuggle drugs out in their suitcases or something?"

"Probably not," Tricia said. "That'd be taking a big chance of getting caught. Mrs. Wong says all the suitcases will be opened at customs on the way home."

Becky said, "Maybe we could ask her if the Hermanns had their tickets for a long time or what."

"Good idea," Melanie replied, shaking off the thought of drug smugglers.

Their cabin's radio speaker crackled. *"The lifeboat drill will now begin. All passengers are required by International Navigational Law to take part in it. Please get your life vests from your cabins and put the vests on, following the instructions on the tags. Next, walk on the stairways to your lifeboat station. Walk. Do not run. Walk. Do not run."*

The voice crackled on as Melanie tied her life vest

around her. With the Hermanns aboard the *Golden Isle*, life vests might not be safe enough.

"We go to Lifeboat Station 30, Golden Deck," Jess said.

"Same as ours," Melanie replied, opening the door. "Probably the same as the Hermanns' too."

"Yipes!" Cara exclaimed.

"Take your cabin keys with you to your lifeboat station," the radio voice interrupted. *"Once you have your life vests on, walk on the stairways to your lifeboat station. . . ."*

Melanie led the way from their cabin, life vest on and ship's map in hand. Behind her, she saw Silvee, William, and Auntie Ying-Ying coming from their cabin, her aunt making them wait while she locked the door.

Unfortunately William yelled another loud, "ABANDON SHIP! ALL PASSENGERS ABANDON SHIP!"

Auntie Ying-Ying swatted at his bottom, just missing. At least it quieted him. No matter how weird he acted, he'd be embarrassed to be spanked in public.

The *Golden Isle*'s staff members lined the stairways. They smiled and hurried passengers along with, "Move along quickly, but do not run."

Melanie and the other TCCers climbed up the two flights of stairs to the Golden Deck. Stepping out on the deck into the sunshine, it was surprising to see so many passengers lining the side of the white ship. They all wore orange life vests, and Melanie's eyes lit on "LIFEBOAT STATION 30" painted on the side of the ship not far from them.

A ship's officer called out, "Men, stand against the ship . . . then the women . . . children in the front."

He glanced at the lifeboat station number stamped on

Melanie's life vest, then at the other TCCers' numbers. "You girls, let the smaller children stand in the first row."

Just then, Silvee, William, and Auntie Ying-Ying arrived.

Melanie crowded up with the others, holding Silvee in front of her. The ship's officer directed William and Auntie Ying-Ying to the middle of the group.

"I'm scared," Silvee said.

"There's nothing to be scared of," Melanie assured her. "It's just a practice. It's an adventure."

Silvee puffed up her face and shook her head.

"Pretend it's a game," Melanie told her. "That's what I'm going to do, just pretend. Anyhow, it's important."

It was a moment before Silvee nodded.

Once everyone lined up, the ship's captain walked down the nearby steps in a fine white uniform and saluted the officer directing them. Next, the captain eyed the Lifeboat 30 passengers. He nodded his approval, then moved on to the next lifeboat group.

While they waited to be dismissed, Melanie looked out at the huge blue ocean. The island of Puerto Rico lay far away now, and there was no land in sight. If the ship went down, they'd *have* to go on the lifeboats to be saved.

Suddenly cables whirred and the lifeboats were lowered, while their officer explained what they'd do if they actually did have to abandon ship. Silvee was right. It was scary.

She held Silvee's shoulders and glanced sideways at the nearby passengers. Everyone looked serious. Her eyes moved on, then stopped at the far edge of the Lifeboat 30 group.

Sid Hermann stared at her angrily.

That was scarier yet.

———————

At long last, everyone returned to their cabins to put away their life vests. Heading through the corridor, Tricia asked, "Did you see Sid Hermann give us the evil eye?"

"I sure did," Melanie replied.

"Where was he?" Becky asked.

"Toward the back of our lifeboat group. Didn't you see him and his family?" Tricia asked.

"Nope," Becky said. "I wasn't looking around much."

"I have a bad feeling that we're going to have to deal with him," Melanie commented.

"Or maybe his grandkids," Tricia answered. "Anyhow, let's make sure they don't sit near us during the cruise director's welcome talk. It's next."

"The *very important* cruise director," Melanie said sarcastically.

Tricia rolled her eyes. "Yeah. Very important."

"How about dinner?" Jess asked. "I'm starved."

"It's supposed to be a *short* talk before dinner," Becky said, "though Maxwell strikes me as long-winded."

In the cabin, Auntie Ying-Ying urged Melanie to go ahead to the Ruby Lounge. "You go with friends. You have work soon on trip."

"All right!" Melanie said.

Before long, she sat with the other TCCers in the Ruby Lounge listening to the *Golden Isle* orchestra play soft music from the front of the room. The Ruby Lounge had red carpeting and rows of chairs and couches around coffee tables. A microphone stood in front by the small dance floor, and on each side of the lounge, big windows looked out to the sea.

"It's sort of an auditorium," Melanie observed.

"Or theater," Tricia replied. "They probably have talent shows and other entertainment right on the dance floor. Maybe we could do a skit."

"Or gymnastics," Jess suggested.

They all laughed, since she was the *only* gymnast among them. By comparison, the rest of them were klutzes.

Before long, Maxwell Thornton hurried up to the orchestra to talk to its leader. He glanced around at the crowd in the Ruby Lounge.

"He dresses nicely," Becky observed. "Sort of show biz."

Melanie noted his navy blue blazer, red-white-and-blue tie, white slacks, and white shoes. The sort of outfit a cruise director was probably expected to wear; it looked perfect for the way he held his chin in the air.

Tricia mimicked him perfectly. *"I'm a very important man on this ship."*

"He thinks he's Mr. Wonderful," Cara said.

"Yep, that's it!" Jess answered. "Mr. Wonderful. The perfect name for him."

"It is," Melanie agreed, "but he'd better not hear us call him that."

"You know it," Becky agreed.

They sat near a door, so they could get to the dining room quickly.

The music stopped, and Melanie glanced around the lounge again. "Don't look now," she warned, "but here comes the Hermann family in the other door."

Luckily, it was a long distance across the crowded room. And even better, Mr. Wonderful had stepped up to the microphone, his phony smile stretching from one ear to the other. He was tall and gangly, and it occurred to Melanie that he might seem klutzy if he didn't think he was so great.

He tapped on the microphone, and the drone of the crowd subsided as they settled back in the chairs and couches. "Ladies and gentlemen," Maxwell announced, "the crew of the *Golden Isle* welcomes you! And I, Maxwell Thornton, your cruise director, welcome you!"

He turned to the orchestra behind him. "This is the *Golden Isle Orchestra* that's been playing that golden-oldie music for you. Let's give them a hand."

Maxwell Thornton applauded with the passengers, and the orchestra men stood up to take a bow. The cruise-line staff, including Steffi, lined up for introductions.

When the orchestra members sat down, Maxwell continued, "I'll introduce our ship's staff briefly, then we'll have the first seating for dinner." He introduced the white-and-navy-blue-uniformed staff with ease.

Everyone from Captain Papas to Sally, the blond fitness person, made a few welcoming remarks. The captain invited passengers to visit the ship's bridge to see how the ship worked . . . Sally told about visiting the ship's gym . . . red-headed Phoebe about shopping in her boutique . . . and other staff members about their departments.

When they'd finished, Maxwell led the applause, then turned back to the passengers. As he looked around the room, his eyes lit on Melanie and the other TCCers. He threw out a hand of welcome. "Ah, there's our Twelve Candles Club, the girls who'll be taking care of your children—"

Taking care of your *children?!* Melanie's mind repeated. Did he mean everyone's children? Every one on the ship's children?! She remembered how scared she was the time she baby-sat six-month-old Pauline Conway. Of course, there probably wouldn't be babies on the ship.

"Stand up, girls," Maxwell urged. He told the other passengers, "You can get to know the Twelve Candles Club girls after dinner in the youth rooms. They're going to make this cruise lots of fun for children ages four through ten. Let's give these brave girls a big hand!"

These brave girls? Melanie's mind echoed again. She didn't feel brave at all, but she rose to her feet with the other TCCers while the staff and passengers applauded.

In the midst of the applause, Melanie felt her eyes drawn across the lounge to the Hermann family. Karla and Jason were applauding, as was their grandmother. But Mr. Sid Hermann was definitely *not* clapping for them.

CHAPTER

5

*B*ells chimed over the Ruby Lounge's loudspeakers. Then a dignified voice said, *"Ladies and gentlemen, dinner is served for those at the first seating."*

Cruise director, Maxwell Thornton, glanced at his huge watch and gave the passengers a big wave. "Folks, we finished the introductions just in time! Now that's what you call perfect timing. . . ."

Folks? Melanie's mind repeated. His "folks" was as fake as his phony ear-to-ear smile.

"Bon appetito!" Maxwell added. "That's Italian for 'have a great appetite.' You guessed it! Somewhere far, far back in my family, I'm Italian."

He laughed. "Now don't forget, our first show here in the Ruby Lounge is after dinner. We'll give you information about the first port, then it's fun, games, and prizes! Best of all, parents and grandparents, the youth rooms will be open for your kiddos tonight."

"You'd think we wouldn't have to sit kids the very first night on the ship," Jess said. "Especially not after spending all day flying here."

Melanie shrugged. "Well, we are getting a free trip. We'll just have to do it . . . and do a good job of it, too."

Over the microphone, Maxwell Thornton added, "If you need a break from your children or they need a break from you, remember the youth rooms open right after the first dinner seating, so you can take the kiddos who are ages four to ten—"

Melanie stood up with the other TCCers, wishing he wouldn't encourage the parents quite so much.

Tricia raised her thick brows. "No matter how we feel about Mr. Wonderful, his timing is perfect."

They started with the crowd for the nearest door.

"He can probably adjust his talks to what's needed," Jess remarked. "I'll bet he could fill an hour or two on any subject. Maybe a whole day or two."

"I heard that he sings, too," Cara said. "And Sally, the fitness instructor, is also a dancer. I guess staff members on cruise ships have to double in lots of roles."

"At least now we know who's who on the ship," Melanie remarked. She studied her ship's map, then tried to figure out where they were and which way to the dining room. She held the map sideways and upside down. "It's sure complicated! We'd better just follow the crowd."

The *Golden Isle* rolled slightly, and she staggered. "Yipes! For a while, I almost forgot we were on a ship. Let's hope we don't get seasick."

"Don't even mention it," Tricia answered. "Let's take the elevator to the dining room."

Melanie glanced out a nearby window as they passed. Whitecaps broke over the inky blue water of the Atlantic Ocean. Nothing but ocean as far as she could see.

Out in the lobby, the elevators were already jammed with passengers on their way to dinner, and the TCCers joined the rest of the crowd on the stairs. Laughing, Melanie held tightly to the handrails as the ship rolled and pitched.

"It's a little scary," Cara said.

"A little," Melanie decided. "But mostly, it feels like an adventure. Mrs. Wong says the water will probably be calmer once we're in the Caribbean Sea."

At the dining room entrance, an elegant headwaiter stood smiling at them. "Good evening," he said politely to Auntie Ying-Ying, Silvee, and William, then included the TCCers. "Your table number, please."

"Table thirty-seven," Melanie's aunt replied. "We all sit at same table."

He turned to a white-jacketed attendant. "Please escort this lovely lady and her charming group to table thirty-seven."

The attendant offered his arm to Auntie Ying-Ying, who took it with pleasure. "This way, if you please," he said to the rest of them, then set out into the festive room.

If you please!? Melanie rolled her eyes at Jess.

"This is big time," Jess laughed.

Smiling, they followed along, winding through the tables. Colorful flags hung from the ceiling, and the endless rows of round tables with white tablecloths were beautifully set. Tall silver vases held red carnations. Other uniformed waiters and busboys hurried around the room, helping to seat passengers.

A waiter, handsome in his black suit and tie, seated Melanie with a showy bow.

"Thank you," she said, feeling as if she were in a movie. His name tag spelled out *Fernando Romero*. "Thank you, Mr. Romero."

The waiter nodded. "Fernando, if you please. I will be your waiter this week. I hope you will enjoy yourselves. May I present your menus?"

Auntie Ying-Ying accepted her menu from him, then looked at the girls. She laughed. "Just like home, huh?"

Melanie almost laughed herself, and William aimed a karate chop at Fernando, who dodged and chuckled.

"William!" Melanie warned. "Aren't you even tired?"

His brown eyes sparkled. "I slept on the planes while you girls talk-talk-talked. I am ready to go-go-go!"

"Well, you're already *here* in case you hadn't noticed."

At least the TCCers and her family fit perfectly at a table for eight people, so William wouldn't annoy other passengers, she thought.

One busboy filled their goblets with tinkling ice water. Another brought a dish of vegie sticks and a basket of freshly baked rolls. Melanie helped herself to a celery stick and munched on it as she eyed the menu. Oysters, caviar, shrimp, lobster, steak, prime rib, fish, roast beef, and lots more.

Too much to choose from. Besides, her eyes kept drifting shut. Holding them open with an effort, she finally decided on a chicken and pasta salad.

Next, Fernando brought everyone soup, then garden salads, and after a while, their main dishes.

Halfway through dinner, Melanie could scarcely raise

her fork to her mouth. She tried to keep her eyelids open but found her head nodding . . . nodding . . . nodding. . . . Suddenly asleep, her chin touched the pasta salad, awakening her. She felt her face turning red.

"Ha-ha-ha!" William laughed loudly. "Ha-ha, ho-ho, Melanie!"

Her friends smiled at her, too. She jerked upright and eyed William. "Ha-ha, ho-ho, yourself!"

Looking around the table, everyone else looked sleepy.

"Jet lag," Auntie Ying-Ying explained.

He muttered to Melanie, "Big deal."

She remembered to answer softly since Dad often said, *A soft word turns away wrath.* "Never mind, William."

He stuck his tongue out at her.

So much for speaking softly, she thought, and concentrated on her food. They were so tired, how could they possibly baby-sit kids tonight?

When dinner finally ended, the TCCers hurried upstairs to the youth rooms on the Royale Deck. In the corridor, they noticed the one-way windows so parents could watch any time. Yipes! They'd have to do a really good job of childcare.

Steffi arrived down the corridor. "Let me show you where stuff is." She led the way into the youth rooms. "The crepe paper, crayons, construction paper, pipe cleaners, and other supplies should be in that top cabinet."

Inside, the rooms looked like Sunday school rooms, except for portholes for windows and three blue gymnastic mats on the floor. Four sets of little tables and chairs would hold twenty-four kids, and bulletin boards hung on the walls, colorful pins stuck in them for displaying artwork.

Steffi opened the cabinet doors, and her mouth dropped open. *Nothing but rolls of white toilet paper!*

"Toilet paper!" Melanie exclaimed with the others.

"A whole cabinet full of it!" Jess added.

Steffi opened cabinet after cabinet, and the rest were empty. A drawer near the sink held stick-on name tags and a felt pen.

Stunned, Steffi held her hands to her face. "Would you believe it? Someone's forgotten to bring the supplies from our closet by the disco. I'm afraid you'll have to manage without them until we get the supply closet key tomorrow morning. On top of that, I have to leave now—"

Five squealing girls raced into the room, two sets of parents hurrying behind them. The girls appeared to be between seven and eight years old—and their breathless parents appeared to be between relief and exhaustion.

"I'll handle it," Tricia offered.

"Good luck!" Steffi called back as she left. "Lots of good luck!"

"Hello, girls," Tricia said. Standing as tall as she could, she announced to them and their parents, "All of us in the Twelve Candles Club have tried to use and learn more about the talents God has given each of us. Do you know what yours might be?"

The girls shook their heads.

"Then we'll give you some ideas," Tricia told them. "Since our art and craft supplies aren't here yet, we'll do something different. For example, Melanie is a model, so she could show the girls how to do modeling. . . ."

All five girls were impressed.

Tricia added, "And Jess is a gymnast, so she can teach

us how to do gymnastics. See, we have these blue mats on the floor so no one will be hurt. And I'm an actress, so we can work on acting. Also, Cara is a writer and Becky is an artist. Becky and Cara, if you'd do name tags for our guests. . . . Or would you girls rather be called Funners? That's what we call the kids we do playcare for at home."

"Funners!" the girls shouted.

The parents left as quickly as the girls' name tags were written.

"What shall we do first?" Tricia asked their new Funners.

"Modeling!" insisted a redhead named Hannah. "We want to do modeling, don't we?"

"Modeling!" answered her equally red-haired cousin, Sarah. "Let's do modeling!"

"Well," Melanie said, "first we begin by practicing good posture. Usually you balance a book on your head . . . but since we don't have books here right now, we'll have to use rolls of toilet paper."

The other TCCers put hands to their lips to keep from laughing, and Melanie knew she didn't dare laugh herself. She grabbed a roll of TP and balanced it tube-side up on top of her head. "Now, girls, put your hands out for balance, then just walk along carefully."

The TCCers helped the girls balance the TP rolls.

"That's it, Hannah! Perfect," Melanie said encouragingly. She told Hannah's redheaded cousin, "That's the way, Sarah. Wow, you two are good at it.

"Take your time, Brittany. No, put it right in the middle of your head. . . ."

Before long, the five Funners balanced the TP rolls on

their heads for a few seconds. Delighted, they began to take chances, then chased the TP rolls around the room when they rolled off.

"Look at me!" the girls shouted. "Look at me!"

Melanie gave a laugh, and her TP roll tumbled from her head, unfurling across the carpet with theirs.

Jess and Becky joined in, TP rolls on top of their heads, arms out for balance.

Just then, three little boys came in. Moments after their parents had signed them in, they joined in balancing TP rolls on their heads, laughing wildly.

The kids whirled and twirled, growing louder and louder, and wilder and wilder.

Becky exclaimed, "I know what we can do! Let's make toilet paper costumes! We could wrap each other up like mummies . . . or even make white wedding dresses."

Little by little, more kids arrived until there were fifteen of them modeling TP, wrapping each other up in it like mummies, or making TP wedding dresses.

"Whoa, Funners!" Jess yelled. "Whoa! Cool it a little!"

"Wrap Melanie like a mummy!" shouted Hannah.

"Okay . . . okay," Melanie answered, too tired to argue. Instead, she turned around and around as they wrapped her in the toilet paper. Dizzy, she suggested, "Let me lie down so you can do my arms and legs."

The other TCCers were being wrapped in toilet paper, too. She stretched out on the carpet and let the kids finish wrapping her arms and legs. Despite the chaos and commotion, her eyelids felt so heavy she could scarcely keep them open. If only she could sleep for one minute . . . or even a few seconds. After all, Becky and Tricia lay stretched out on the carpet now, too. . . .

Suddenly she heard a distant "Hiii-ee-yah!"

"Melanie. . . !" Silvee called out, her face peeking out from a toilet paper bonnet. "Wake up, Melanie, wake up! Look at my wedding dress! Why are you sleeping on the floor?"

When Melanie opened her eyes, the youth room whirled like a nightmare. When the room stopped, she realized the sight before her was real. The other TCCers, some wrapped in toilet paper, lay half asleep near the walls, too. And, in the middle of the room, William was teaching the Funners to karate chop each other, yelling "Hiii-ee-yah! Hiii-ee-yah!"

Worse yet, Auntie Ying-Ying had joined in, also wrapped in toilet paper. When her aunt saw she was awake, she said, "You so tired, Melanie, we let you sleep a little."

Before Melanie could shake herself awake, the door burst open. Maxwell Thornton stood before them, an angry frown creasing his face.

Maxwell yelled, "This room is out of control! Obviously twelve-year-old girls can't handle a youth program."

"Melanie, wake up!" Silvee urged again.

Melanie cringed and closed her eyes. "I don't think I want to."

———

The next morning, she opened her eyes and hoped the toilet paper disaster had been a nightmare.

No . . . the ship was moving, its engines humming.

She glanced around. She was definitely in the cabin. Silvee breathed softly on the fold-out bed beside her, and

Auntie Ying-Ying stepped from the bathroom, already wearing a red pants outfit.

Melanie closed her eyes, pretending to sleep. But blotting out the present only brought back the memories of last night's disaster.

Furious, Maxwell Thornton had taken charge. He'd growled, "If you kids don't behave, I'll report you to your parents—and that'll be the end of the youth program for you."

His anger quieted everyone.

Stalking around the room, he snarled, "It looks like a snowstorm hit! Clean the room this minute! I'll stand right here and make sure you pick up every speck of the toilet tissue. *Every* speck. NOW!"

The TCCers and Funners had set to work fast.

Luckily, before he could start yelling again, parents had begun to arrive to pick up their kids. And finally the evening's youth program had ended.

Maxwell gave the TCCers one last angry message. "We expect you girls to keep order here. ORDER! These kids were out of control—and it better not happen again!"

He hadn't been one bit like the jolly cruise director at the welcoming talk. It was as if he had two opposite personalities. Melanie remembered her dad saying that happened to people on drugs—

Could Mr. Wonderful possibly be on drugs?

Melanie sat up in bed, remembering Tricia telling them about drugs being brought in through the Caribbean.

No, it wouldn't happen on their ship. No way!

Lately, she'd begun to pray the moment she awoke—and her days seemed better for it when she did. At the rate things were going, she'd better pray now.

Lord, please give us a quiet day today! And if it can't be quiet, please show us what to do!

What should she wear? Maybe her new white top and pants, and a cotton sweater because of the icy air-conditioning.

Dressed, she headed down the corridor to the back— oops, to the *stern*—of the ship. Last night after the youth program, the TCCers had at least taken time to check out the different decks and public rooms on the ship. They'd also decided to meet for breakfast outside on the Royale Deck, near the children's pool.

Melanie made her way toward the doors, passing through a small lounge that served light buffet breakfasts. She'd see if the others were out on deck, then come back. Stepping through the doors, she stopped in amazement.

The sea was turquoise!

Not inky blue with whitecaps, but turquoise as shown in the Caribbean travel brochure. A soft, warm breeze lifted her hair slightly, and she strolled to the railing. The sight of the beautiful white *Golden Isle* surrounded by the turquoise sea was . . . unreal. Absolutely unreal.

After a moment, she remembered the TCCers. She glanced at the semicircle of umbrella tables and chairs around the children's Royale Pool, then to the rows of chaise lounges. Passengers already occupied a few of them—eating, reading, or lounging in the sunshine. At the far end, Cara sat on a lounge and wrote in her journal, probably about their shipboard Funners and the Great Toilet Paper Disaster.

Melanie made her way through the chaise lounges and

umbrella tables. "How about this turquoise water!"

"I've been trying to describe the sea in my journal," Cara replied. "I can't decide if the word for its color is glorious or awesome."

"Both," Melanie decided. "Where's everyone else?"

"On their way," Cara answered. "I was the first one up and thought I'd give them more room to dress. How about your family?"

"Auntie Ying-Ying was helping Silvee dress when I left. William was still snoring. They're going to eat in the dining room. William likes eggs, pancakes, sausages, and all. You know, the works."

"I ate out here," Cara told her. "Orange juice, cereal, and a muffin."

Melanie tossed her sweater on the empty lounge by Cara's. "Think that's what I'll do. You want me to get anything else for you?"

Cara smiled sheepishly. "Maybe I'll have another cranberry muffin. We'll need plenty of energy to sit those Funners."

Melanie smiled herself. "Probably." She added, "I prayed for a quiet day."

"Me too. Last night was wild, but sitting here and looking out at the sea makes it worth it."

Melanie glanced out again. "It does. And we'll have the whole afternoon on shore without Funners. Guess I'll go to the buffet now."

"I'll get us an umbrella table," Cara said. "The others should be here any minute, and it'll be easier than eating on a lounge chair."

Inside, Melanie grabbed a cafeteria tray. She'd no more

than started in line than Jess, Becky, and Tricia appeared. "We can eat on the deck or in the dining room," she told them, "but Cara is saving us an umbrella table by the pool."

"Definitely outside for me," Jess answered, lining up, too.

"Steffi gave us a call," Becky told Melanie. "She wants Jess and you to get the supply closet key from the registration desk, then bring the boxes of stuff up for the week."

"Why the two of us?" Melanie asked.

Jess laughed. "Because we're the shortest! She says she's taking pity on us because she's always been short, too."

"Weird idea," Melanie answered.

"No weirder than Maxwell Thornton," Jess replied. "I thought Mr. Wonderful might really lose it last night."

Melanie recalled his anger. "So did I. He acted so different. I thought . . . maybe he was on drugs."

"Drugs!" Jess repeated. "You really think so?!"

Melanie shrugged. "Maybe. He seems sort of, you know . . . my dad would call it neurotic. Kind of mentally unstable." Suddenly she saw last night's waiter—Fernando—at work behind the buffet counter. Fernando was not only adding a tray of fresh muffins to the buffet, but he was listening intently.

Melanie spoke up so he would hear. "We're probably wrong about that. W-a-y w-r-o-n-g about anyone being on drugs. Definitely v-e-r-y w-r-o-n-g about it."

Jess darted an odd glance at her, not understanding. "What worries me is that Mr. Wonderful might be right about one thing. Maybe we're not up to the job of caring for so many kids for a whole week."

Melanie drew a deep breath. "Thank goodness! At least I'm not the only one wondering about that!"

CHAPTER

6

The TCCers ate breakfast at an umbrella table near the children's pool. Two of their new Funners eyed them from nearby lounges, then jumped up and ran over.

Red-haired Hannah asked, "When do we start the youth program? When, huh? When?"

"Nine o'clock," Melanie answered. She glanced at her watch. "About fifteen more minutes."

Sarah cozied up to Melanie, her green eyes sparkling. "Please, can we play mummies again?"

"No way!" Melanie answered, then softened her tone. "What I mean is no more wild stuff. First, we'll get you all settled, and Tricia will take you on a Magic Carpet Ride. Jess and I have to get supplies so we can draw and do craft things."

"Can we stay with you now?" Hannah asked. "Can we?"

"*May* we?" Melanie corrected.

Sarah and Hannah begged together. "May we? May we?"

They reminded Melanie of Silvee. "You may, I guess."

"Where's Silvee and William?" Hannah asked.

"We like them," Sarah put in.

"We like Silvee and William," Hannah added. "Most of all, we like karate chops."

Melanie didn't even want to think about all of those Funners karate chopping again. "Silvee and William are eating breakfast with our aunt down in the dining room."

Sarah asked, "Why does your family have peeky eyes?"

Peeky eyes?!

Melanie clenched her fists. "Do you mean our eyes seem more slanted than yours?"

"Yes," Sarah replied. "Peeky-slanty eyes. Why do you and Silvee and William have peeky-slanty eyes?"

Melanie tried to smile. "Because my family came from China many, many years ago. Asian people often have slanty eyes, but we are Americans—"

"They're nice eyes," Sarah said. "Hannah and I have cat-green, big-as-bugs' eyes. We don't like them."

Melanie's heart softened, and she gave her a hug. "Green eyes are very beautiful. Especially on girls with red hair like yours."

"Don't like our red hair, either," Sarah complained.

"It's very nice," Melanie assured them. "See, our friend Tricia has reddish blond hair. Isn't it beautiful?"

"Ours isn't like hers," Sarah complained.

"Ours is like carrots," Hannah added. "Ug-ug-ugly orange."

Just then, a crowd of walkers bore down on them, led by

Sally, the fitness person. "Step it up! Step it up!" she called cheerily, and everyone moved out of their path.

That was one way to move people out of the way, Melanie thought. Maybe they could walk their new Funners around the deck for an activity, too.

Becky stood up. "Like it or not, guys, it's time to get to the youth room."

"Can we go with you?" Hannah begged. "Can we? Can we?"

Melanie decided not to correct them again. "Your parents have to check you in and out of the youth rooms. It's a rule."

Hannah scrunched up her face. "Okay," she said unhappily.

Sarah turned, karate chopping the air. "Hiii-ee-yah! Hiii-ee-yah! Hiii-ee-yah!"

"Hiii-ee-yah!" Hannah echoed, chopping the air herself.

Melanie crossed her eyes as the two of them karate chopped their way across the deck to their parents. "Look at what William has started. We'll have a whole week of it!"

"I wonder if those girls are actually from Santa Rosita," Jess remarked. "We didn't see them on the planes or anything."

"Yiiii!" Melanie exclaimed. "You know, Maxwell Thornton did make it sound like the youth room was open to everyone on the ship. I meant to find out about it—"

"We'd better find out today," Becky said.

At nine o'clock, when they arrived outside the youth room door, lots of kids waited with Auntie Ying-Ying in the corridor. "Only forty-five kids on ship," she called out.

"Forty-five kids!" the TCCers echoed.

Auntie Ying-Ying nodded. "They not here all the time, and I help. You see . . . we have big fun."

Melanie protested, "No one told us we'd have to take care of all of the ship's kids. No one until Maxwell Thornton mentioned it last night."

"Misunderstanding," Auntie replied. "Mrs. Wong says you supposed to take care of all kids. They not here all the time, and I help. . . ."

It sounded to Melanie as if it were all arranged. She turned to her aunt. "Mrs. Wong should have gotten it straight from the beginning, before she even asked us."

Auntie Ying-Ying nodded. "You right, but it be okay. You see."

Steffi hurried around the corner from the elevators.

"I've got the key to the youth rooms," Steffi assured them. "Also, loads of pens and name tags. Wish I could stay, but I have to help sell shore excursion tickets at the purser's office." Steffi unlocked the door. "Melanie and Jess, you'll have to go to the registration desk."

Just then, Mrs. Wong arrived.

Melanie called the kids over to her. "Aren't we supposed to just sit Santa Rosita kids?"

Mrs. Wong raised her brows unhappily. "I'm sorry about the misunderstanding. The cruise line people expect you to sit all children between ages four and ten. I'm truly sorry."

Steffi called back, "Jess and Melanie, don't forget the supply closet stuff as soon as the kids are name-tagged."

Melanie nodded, and Jess said, "We got your message. Believe me, we'll be glad to escape from this bunch."

Steffi waved them down laughingly. "See you!" she added and started to rush off.

Inside the youth rooms, Becky took charge. "First, everyone fill out your name tags. Write your cabin number on them, so we can call your parents if we need to. Once you're all ready, Tricia will take us on a Magic Carpet Ride."

"Our own Pirates of the Caribbean," Tricia put in. "How many of you have seen the Pirates of the Caribbean attraction at Disneyland or maybe at Disney World?"

Lots of kids' hands went up.

"The Caribbean used to be full of pirates," Tricia told them. "Maybe we'll scout some out this week."

At least the kids listened and appeared interested.

Becky explained to the Funners, "Tricia is an actress. She acts in lots of plays and skits, so you know it will be good. Be sure to get your name tags on, so I'll know who can help me fight the pirates."

At a kid-sized table, Melanie and Jess showed the younger Funners how to write their names on paper tags. Nearby, other children helped Tricia lay out a "magic carpet" of white toilet paper curving through the youth room.

"We have a real magic carpet at home," Tricia told them, "but *here* we're in the Caribbean, right where pirates lived."

Melanie rolled her eyes at Cara. "If only we had that raggedy brown rug with us. Already there are thirty kids."

"Tricia can pull it off till we're back with the supplies." Cara lowered her voice, "Look who's coming in to join us!"

Karla and Jason Hermann stood in the doorway.

Melanie whispered, "I can't believe it!"

As usual, ten-year-old Karla wore a smug expression, as if she were terribly important. But Jason gave them a hopeful, front-tooth-missing smile.

Realizing she was the TCC member standing closest to

them, Melanie forced a smile. "Hi, guys!" she said, trying to sound confident. "Welcome to the youth room."

Karla shot her a glance that asked, "Are you kidding?" But Jason answered with an excited, "Hi!"

To her surprise, Melanie found herself asking, "How did you happen to come on the cruise?"

Jason's face fell. "Our grandparents got our parents' tickets because they're—"

Karla elbowed him hard.

. . . *because they're in jail*, Melanie thought. *Because their parents and aunt and uncle are in jail!*

Karla quickly threw in, "We heard you toilet-papered the youth rooms last night. Sounds babyish to me."

Melanie ignored the comment. "We're just leaving for the supply closet. We'll have lots of craft stuff."

"I don't like crafts, either," Karla complained. "Our grandparents made us come here."

Melanie thought fast. "Tricia's an actress. She comes up with lots of acting games. Do you like acting?"

Karla brightened. "Maybe."

"Hey, Karla and Jason!" Tricia called out. "Hop on our 'magic carpet' for a ride to a pirate island!"

Karla raised her chin snootily, but Jason said, "Pirates, Karla! Come on, let's go!"

Melanie called out behind her, "Jess and I are going for supplies now."

They rushed to the nearest elevator, which promptly opened and was actually empty. Inside, a metal panel gave the names of the floors and a few additional listings. One was clearly marked REGISTRATION; another, DISCO.

"We'd better get another map of the ship or we'll never

find anything," Melanie remarked.

"I'll get a map while you get the key," Jess said.

They felt the elevator moving down while the *Golden Isle* moved forward. "Could you believe Karla and Jason Hermann coming for the youth program?" Jess asked.

Melanie shrugged. "I don't know, but maybe God has something to do with it."

Moments later, they stepped out and found the registration desk just around the corner. Steffi was selling shore excursion tickets in one of the long lines, but she was too busy to notice them. As they hurried along, it struck Melanie that all of the cruise staff members seemed to have great tans and big white smiles.

Jess headed toward the information counter to pick up extra maps of the ship, and Melanie stepped up to the registration desk. "I'm supposed to pick up the key for the youth room supply closet."

Steffi must have alerted the blond registration clerk because he wasn't surprised. "So you're part of the youth program crew."

"We are," Melanie answered.

She noticed that his name tag said "Ted," and he had a deep dimple in his chin.

He handed over the key. "Don't forget to return it. With so many passengers arriving and departing every week, keys have a way of disappearing."

"Thanks. I won't forget."

Suddenly she felt uneasy. "Is this the only key for the closet?"

He glanced at a board with keys hanging on hooks. "Yep. Looks like it must be. The closet is easy to find, down by the disco on the Ocean Deck."

"I haven't seen the disco yet," she admitted.

"It doesn't open until late at night," the clerk replied. "All the late-night dancers are probably still sleeping now."

As Melanie thanked him, Jess joined her at the counter with two maps of the ship.

"Take the middle elevators," Ted suggested. "They're the only ones that go down to the Ocean Deck. Go to the right, pass the boutique, then ride those elevators down."

"Thanks," Melanie answered almost in unison with Jess.

Moments later, they stepped out of the elevator and onto the Ocean Deck. In the corridor, small metal signs spelled out, THEATER, DISCO, and CREW CABINS ONLY. Indented arrows pointed out the directions to take.

"The supply closet must be to the right," Melanie said.

As they started up the dimly lit corridor, Jess remarked, "It's spooky down here without crew or passengers around."

Melanie hurried along behind her. "No portholes to let in light, either, and lots of engine noise. It'd be hard to sleep in the crew cabins down here."

"Maybe they get used to it," Jess replied.

The engines made a low, rumbly roar, and the ship vibrated here, too. According to the map, this was the center of the ship's bottom deck.

Melanie spotted a door with a sign that said SUPPLY CLOSET, CREW ONLY. "That's it." She smiled. "I guess we're crew now."

"And there's the disco's door," Jess replied. "Should we see if we can peek in?"

Melanie tried the knob. "It's unlocked."

Opening the door, they peered in.

Black curtains circled the room . . . a large ball covered with small mirrored squares hung from the ceiling . . . black carpeting. . . . Spotlights pointed at the mirrored ceiling ball, but the only light on now came from a dim bulb mounted between the open curtains on the far wall by a cargo door.

"Eerie," Melanie whispered as they stepped in. It smelled musty, like stale cigarette smoke.

Jess nodded. "Looks like a place for night people, all right. Look at the dirty ashtrays."

Melanie felt nervous. "We'd better get out of here and get the supplies—"

Men's voices filtered down the hallway, growing louder.

Panicked, Melanie and Jess stared at each other. What if they were found snooping around, especially after last night's TP disaster?

Jess hissed, "Close the door!"

Melanie closed it more quickly than quietly, glad for the loud engine noise. "Hurry! Hide!"

"Behind the curtains!"

They ducked behind the nearest black curtain and edged to the left, finding a cramped storage corner. The black curtains curved around for the disco, leaving corners for storage.

As Melanie's eyes grew accustomed to the darkness, she slapped a hand over her mouth.

Yiiiiii! Coffins! The hair on the back of her neck prickled, as if it stood straight up.

One . . . two . . . three. . . .

Three coffins stacked in their corner. . . !

Jess grabbed her arm in shock.

Hadn't Steffi told them that coffins were put on last so they could be taken off first? These were deep inside the ship. Melanie drew a deep breath. They'd have to lean back against the coffins. She shuddered, hoping they were empty!

The disco door opened and a rough voice demanded, "You sure the coast is clear?"

"Yep, no one here," a second voice answered. "Strange. This door's supposed to be kept locked until nine tonight."

"It wasn't locked now!" the rough voice returned angrily. "I thought you had everything under control—"

"Probably some new crewman forgot," said the second voice. "You can't depend on anyone anymore."

"I don't like it," argued the raspy voice. "Looks like a risky situation. If there's one thing I hate, it's taking unnecessary risks."

To Melanie's relief, the voices moved to the right.

Her heart pounded hard, and Jess's fingers dug into her arm. Worse, now as the ship rolled, the black curtains parted slightly. Before she could shut them, she saw Sid Hermann with two other men looking in the right-hand corner.

"I want this stuff outta here *now*," Sid Hermann announced.

What stuff? Melanie wondered in terror.

"Don't like it at all," he continued in his rough voice. "Dancers could bash right into them. I looked in around midnight, and the dancing was wild."

"There's no other place for it," replied the second voice. The voice sounded a lot like . . . no, it *was* Maxwell Thornton! "The ship's cargo space is jammed."

Sid Hermann asked, "Then how do you expect to load the stuff in them?"

"Stuff" must mean "drugs," Melanie thought.

The third man said, "As long as I got charge of the kitchen, I can get anything moved around the ship. *Anything at all!* Don't worry about it."

Maxwell Thornton warned, "Just so they're kept locked."

"They'll be kept locked," the kitchen man assured them.

Sid Hermann grumbled, "I don't like the feel of this room . . . this disco." His voice grew louder and closer to Melanie and Jess. "I got a sixth sense about places, and believe me, this disco don't feel good."

Melanie pressed back, bumping the coffins.

"What's that?" Sid Hermann barked.

Melanie froze, though she still shook inside.

Beside her, she thought Jess had stopped breathing.

"Just cracking and creaking in the ship," Maxwell answered. "These older tubs are noisy. Let's go up. Mr. Hermann, we're honored you'd come along in person—"

"Honored!" Sid Hermann rasped. "Wasn't much choice. The ones supposed to come are locked up! The lawyers couldn't spring 'em. Seems like I always got to do other people's jobs for 'em."

The door closed behind them, and their voices drifted off down the corridor.

Melanie let out her breath. "Drugs!" she whispered. "They must be smuggling drugs!" She felt as horrified as Jess looked in the dim light. "The question is, what can we do about it?"

CHAPTER

7

Melanie and Jess raced back to the youth room, carrying boxes of supplies. As they rounded the corridor, they could already hear the kids in an uproar.

"Oh no! Wonder what they've been doing?" Melanie asked.

"I'm afraid we're about to find out!" Jess answered.

As soon as they rushed through the youth room door, Becky demanded, "Where were you guys? We've got forty kids here! We're about to go crazy!"

Jess began, "You won't believe what happened—"

"We'll tell you later," Melanie finished for her. As it was, Karla Hermann watched them, but then so did the others. Melanie plopped her box of supplies on a table. "There's lots of stuff for making costumes. Enough black cloth for an army . . . eye patches and plastic swords. Guess pirates have always been big here in the Caribbean."

"Hear that, Funners?" Tricia asked the kids. "We can make costumes for Costume Night. How many want to be pirates?"

"Yeah, pirates!" most of them yelled, stampeding through the room to the boxes.

Becky sorted through a box. "All right! Lots of crayons, scissors, crepe paper, construction paper, and stuff. Even pirate hat patterns."

Tricia called out, "Costume party, here we come!"

Cara stepped out of the kids' way and joined Melanie. "What kept you and Jess so long?"

"Tell you later," Melanie answered.

Cara darted a curious look at her but asked no more.

Melanie glanced around the room. No toilet paper mummies this morning, but plenty of white toilet paper flowers, bracelets, necklaces, and other creations. "Hmmm. You put the rest of the toilet paper to good use."

"I think we've used every piece of it, too," Cara answered. "Luckily Steffi had someone bring us pipe cleaners, so we weren't as limited as last night."

"What else did you do?"

"Tricia started with the Magic Carpet Ride," Cara replied. "They liked that, but it only ate up fifteen minutes. You guys must have been gone a whole hour."

"Believe me, it wasn't a fun outing," Jess said. "Come on, we'd better help with costume making."

In her presidential voice, Becky announced, "I'm going to organize you Funners into five groups. Nine Funners to a group. Each TCCer takes charge of one table. Melanie, the table in the back room . . . Jess, the kids on the floor back there . . . Cara, this table. . . . Kids, please pick a table and take your supplies with you."

Sarah yelled, "I want Melanie's table—"

"We want Melanie! We want Melanie!" Hannah agreed.

Becky announced, "Sarah and Hannah to Melanie's table."

"Me too!" Silvee added.

"And Silvee," Becky agreed.

William cut the air with a karate chop, yelled a wild "Hiii-ee-yah!" and joined them without asking permission.

Melanie asked him, "Where's Auntie Ying-Ying?"

He grinned. "Out on the deck sleeping."

Silvee huffed, "Auntie's reading a book!"

Next came Karla and Jason Hermann.

"Great!" Melanie said, though she wasn't so sure.

Becky assigned three other boys to her for a total of nine. Melanie read the boys' names. "Kip, Jake, and Bunky. What good names!"

They grinned as if they didn't quite believe her.

"How old are you?" she asked, guessing maybe ten.

"Twenty years old," Kip answered.

"I'm forty," Jake said.

Bunky put in, "Two hundred and fifty years old."

Melanie laughed. "You sure have good imaginations." She directed them to the back room. "Take your materials. I'll get one of those bolts of black fabric for us."

When she arrived at her table, the kids were fighting over chairs. The boys did not want to sit by the girls, except for Jason Hermann, who stayed close to his older sister, Karla.

Melanie sat down on a corner of the table. "Well, kiddos, how many of you want to make peg legs for your pirate costumes?"

"Peg legs?" Kip asked. "How can we walk on a peg leg?"

"What is it?" Hannah asked. "What's a peg leg?"

"It's a wooden leg, usually for people who have a missing lower leg," Melanie explained. "It'd be hard to walk on, all right. Maybe that's why some pirates were grouchy."

Everyone laughed a little.

Melanie continued, "If we make long black pirate coats, we just need a bright, shiny peg leg drawn on black construction paper. We can use white or silvery crayons to draw it."

"Or yellow!" Silvee suggested.

William rolled his eyes toward the ceiling. "Who ever heard of a *yellow* peg leg?!"

Melanie sent him a look. "It can be any color we choose, William. Come on, Funners, we're supposed to have fun, so let's get going on these costumes."

They settled down to work at the table.

"Is the costume party tonight?" Hannah asked.

Melanie tried to remember the details from today's ship's newspaper. "Ummm . . . tonight's the Captain's Gala Dinner, which means very dressed up. And the costume party is our last night on the ship."

"Where are we going after lunch?" Sarah inquired.

"Tortula. Maybe I have the booklet." She dug in her pocket. "Believe it or not, here it is!"

She read off their stops from the front page. "Today, we stop at Tortola . . . tomorrow, Antigua . . . then Martinique, Barbados, and St. Thomas."

She opened to the first page. "Here's today's stop. 'The peaceful island of Tortola boasts unspoiled beaches, turquoise waters, and charming people. Head for Cane Garden Bay on the north coast for swimming. On your way there, you'll pass the overgrown ruins of huge sugarcane plantations and remnants of forts from the days when pirates ruled the seas. Or take a glass-bottomed boat tour to look at the beautiful coral reefs.' "

"Pirates!" William yelled. "Hiii-ee-yah!"

The other boys joined in. "Pirates! Pirates!"

Just then, Maxwell Thornton stuck his head in the room, smiling like Mr. Wonderful. "Do I hear children having fun?"

Only a few of the Funners cheered, probably because his nasty self had scared most of them last night.

"Great!" he said with his phony smile. "We want you to have a great time. We want you to sail on the *Golden Isle* again and again." Having said that, he rushed off.

Good riddance, Melanie thought.

Just before noon, Auntie Ying-Ying rushed in. "Time for Funners to wash up for lunch," she announced. "Your parents will be here to take you."

She blinked and put on her sunglasses. It appeared she'd been sleeping, all right, Melanie thought. Probably the sunshine and the ship's movement made her drowsy. A good thing she hadn't been along for the coffins-in-the-disco and the drug-smuggling discovery.

Melanie drew a deep breath. At lunch, she and Jess would have to tell Cara, Tricia, and Becky what they'd learned in the disco.

———

When the youth program ended, Melanie rushed off to return the supply closet key. She tried to think how to ask the registration clerk, Ted, innocent-sounding questions.

Thank goodness he was still at the registration desk. She put the supply room key on the desk. "Ummm . . . you said keys are always disappearing," she said. "Does that mean someone who isn't supposed to could get into our cabin?"

Ted smiled, the dimple in his chin deepening. "Not likely. The cabin stewards keep a good eye out on the cabins." He hesitated in concern. "Why? Is something missing from yours?"

"No, nothing," Melanie answered quickly. "I was just wondering. My family was robbed once, so we try to be careful. Anyhow, thanks for helping us get the supplies."

"Did you find everything you need?" he asked.

"Yep. There's plenty of stuff for the kids. Thanks again. Gotta get going for lunch." She smiled and hurried away, hoping she hadn't aroused his suspicions.

At twelve-thirty, the green island of Tortola rose from the sea in the distance.

"Beautiful Tortola!" Maxwell Thornton boomed over the loudspeakers. *"Isn't it an incredible sight? It's said to have been the fiercest pirate island in the Caribbean."*

"It's beautiful, all right," Melanie said. She and the other TCCers ate lunch at an umbrella table on the deck. "It'd be more incredible if he didn't inform everyone of it."

Other passengers hurried to the railings to look at the island, but the TCCers' discussion of the disco discovery was too important to worry about sightseeing.

Tricia's green eyes bulged. "You mean you actually saw Sid Hermann and Maxwell Thornton?"

"We did," Melanie answered, "but we didn't see the man in charge of the kitchen. Mostly, we hid behind the disco curtain and heard them talk."

"And shook like crazy up against those creepy coffins," Jess added.

Melanie nodded. "That's the truth."

"What do we do about it?" Tricia asked.

"Tell a responsible adult," Jess answered. "Everyone always says, 'tell a responsible adult.' "

"Auntie Ying-Ying's the adult with us," Melanie answered, "and let's face it, she's not always so responsible."

Jess said, "If we phone home from the ship's office, people will hear us. If we send a FAX home, crew members will see it and maybe tell Maxwell."

"All right," Melanie agreed. "I'll tell Auntie as soon as I get her away from that crowd by the railing." The crowd included Silvee and William. Besides that, her aunt had her camcorder and was filming like crazy.

The moment Melanie arrived at the railing, Auntie Ying-Ying zoomed the camera in at her. When she'd finished, she announced to nearby passengers, "This is niece, Melanie Lin. Melanie was model . . . New York City model before we move to California. She model for Coca-Cola, IBM, and other big company. Very important model."

The passengers raised their brows. Some wanted to know how to get modeling jobs for themselves or for members of their families.

"Our ship will be docking at Tortola in five minutes," Maxwell spoke over the loudspeakers. *"Be sure to take your boarding card."*

Auntie Ying-Ying called out, "Get in line! Get in line! Be back soon. Silvee, come! Let's go to the bathroom! Melanie, you want to go to the b-a-t-h-r-o-o-m?"

Melanie felt heat rush to her face. "No, thanks."

Something like this would happen if she told her aunt about what happened in the disco, Melanie thought. Auntie Ying-Ying would broadcast the news without thinking and ruin any chance of catching the bad guys.

Melanie got in line with the TCCers.

"Did you tell her?" Becky asked.

Melanie shook her head. "It's impossible. She'd tell everyone on the ship."

They stared at each other, then nodded gloomily.

"What about Mrs. Wong?" Cara suggested.

"We don't really know her," Becky answered. "She'd probably think we're just over-imaginative kids."

Jess pressed her lips together. "Maybe I could FAX the FBI man who helped you, Tricia. Dad has that FAX in our home office, and I could use some kind of a coded message."

"Like what?" Tricia asked.

Melanie had a brainstorm. "Do an address like to Mr. Smith, in care of Mr. and Mrs. Bennett."

"Yeah!" Jess agreed. "My parents would take it right to the Bennetts'. That's perfect!"

The line of passengers edged to the gangway.

"We can work on the rest of it later," Melanie decided.

Just then, Auntie Ying-Ying arrived with Silvee. "Hurry! Get off ship! Buses go without us!"

On the tour bus, they looked out at green, jungly scenery; sugarcane plantation ruins; and broken-down forts from pirate days. It was incredible, all right, Melanie thought. Incredible.

Later, at the beach, Maxwell Thornton strolled along

the water with other crew members. "Hey, TCCers!" he yelled. "How's it going?"

"Fine, thanks!" they answered.

Maxwell seemed to be everywhere, even when they swam. "Hey, kiddos!" he called to them. "Nice swimming."

Melanie swam away slowly in the warm, turquoise water. Jess swam beside her. "You think he's on to us?"

"Maybe he has to keep track of passengers."

"I don't like the way he looks at us," Melanie said.

"Maybe he doesn't like the way we look at him, either."

When they returned to the *Golden Isle*, he stood welcoming everyone aboard. "A wonderful island, isn't it?" he asked them. "Yes! Wonderful!"

Suddenly Melanie remembered what he'd said about moving the coffins after the first port. Someone else would have had to move them since Maxwell had been on the island. Maybe the man from the kitchen.

———

At six o'clock that evening, Auntie Ying-Ying led their family through the ship toward the Ruby Lounge. Auntie wore her long, red sequined gown. "All smile big when we get to camera," she told Silvee, William, and Melanie. "We look nice for pictures."

So they did, Melanie thought. She and Silvee wore white lacy dresses; William wore his dark blue suit. The passengers in line were nicely dressed, too—the men in dark suits or black tuxedos, the women in stunning dresses or evening gowns.

It seemed as if they were in a grand hotel, except for the turquoise sea outside the ship's windows, and the feel of the

Golden Isle's steady movement.

As they moved forward in line, they neared Sally, the blond fitness director, who looked glamorous in a black gown. Smiling, she said, "Please fill out these name tags. We want to know your names."

Melanie wrote Silvee's name tag and stuck the tag onto her dress, then did her own.

Ahead, inside the Ruby Lounge, cameras flashed as the ship's photographer took pictures. Melanie and her family edged forward in the line of passengers to meet the captain and have their pictures taken with him.

She'd tell the captain what she'd heard in the disco, Melanie thought. After all, he was in charge of the ship.

A new thought struck.

What if he knew about the smuggling? And what if he was in on it himself?

Just then, Maxwell stepped toward them. He wore a black tuxedo, white shirt, a sequined red-and-white bow tie—and his usual ear-to-ear smile.

"Don't you all look wonderful!" he gushed. "Just wonderful! Now, be sure to put on your best smile for your picture. Steffi will introduce you to Captain Papas, then the photographer will take your picture. And remember, no youth room work tonight, since you did it this morning. You may want to sit with the kids for the entertainment tonight."

Sure enough, Steffi stood ahead of them wearing a white gown and a fabulous diamond necklace. Probably fake diamonds unless she had lots and lots of money. Beside her stood the captain in a splendid white uniform.

Suddenly it was their turn to move forward.

Steffi said, "Captain Papas, may I present Mrs. Lin and

her family . . . Silvee Lin, William Lin, and Melanie Lin."

The captain smiled broadly. "A pleasure to meet you," he remarked as he shook hands with each of them.

No, best *not* to tell him about the drug smuggling, Melanie decided. At least not in this line of passengers.

Maxwell arranged her family for the group picture with the captain.

"That's perfect," the photographer gushed as his camera flashed. "You all look wonderful. Just wonderful." He sounded like Maxwell.

As their eyes recovered from the flare of light, a uniformed staff member motioned them toward the seating area of the vast Ruby Lounge. "Enjoy the party," he told them. "Our waiters are serving drinks and hors d'oeuvres."

But Melanie heard the captain repeat to the people behind them: "A pleasure to meet you." He probably wouldn't even remember their names, she thought. It was *not* reassuring.

She glanced back.

Even less reassuring was the sight of the Hermanns coming through the line—and just a few families behind her! Karla raised her chin when she saw her, but Jason grinned, friendly as ever.

Just then, Maxwell remarked rather loudly, "Beautiful jewelry, Mrs. Hermann. Very beautiful."

Mrs. Hermann smiled, and her husband said gruffly, "That necklace and those earrings are diamonds. Not fake stuff like some passengers on this ship wear."

"Be sure to use the ship's safe," Maxwell told him.

"Not on your life!" Mr. Hermann shot back. "We heard of jewelry missing from that safe already."

Auntie Ying-Ying had moved forward into the vast lounge with Silvee and William. Now her aunt glanced back at Melanie. "What you do there, Melanie? Not good manners to listen other people talk!"

Melanie rushed on into the Ruby Lounge, hoping the Hermanns hadn't heard. Maybe the orchestra's music had drowned out her aunt's words.

Jewelry missing from the ship's safe—and drug smuggling! Was there some sort of connection?

When they sat down in the Ruby Lounge, she turned her attention to the ship's orchestra. Its members were older men, but every one of them suddenly struck her as suspect. Maybe even Steffi was in on the drug smuggling.

A waiter stopped by with drinks. Melanie accepted a Coke and took a cooling sip. Another waiter arrived with tiny sandwiches and meatballs speared with toothpicks. She took a meatball. Delicious. She decided that everything about the cruise would be wonderful if only she hadn't heard the men in the disco this morning.

Before long, the other TCCers joined them, all dressed up. Jess in a white satiny suit; Cara wore a creamy yellow dress; Becky, sapphire blue; and Tricia, seafoam green.

Jess sat down beside Melanie. "Nice tonight, huh?"

Melanie nodded. She'd tell them what she'd heard about the stolen jewelry later.

"It took forever for us to get dressed up together," Cara said. "A good thing you went ahead."

"I thought about telling the captain you-know-what," Melanie told them.

Auntie Ying-Ying's eyes caught hers. "Tell captain what?"

"A secret," Melanie decided to answer. "Just a secret."

Luckily, her aunt seemed satisfied.

Before long, the ship's dinner bell rang, and Maxwell's voice boomed over the loudspeakers, *"Dinner is served for the first seating. Bon appetito!"*

"Old Mr. Wonderful is everywhere, isn't he?" Becky asked as they rose to their feet.

Melanie nodded. "He's everywhere, all right."

Auntie Ying-Ying shot her another curious glance before turning her attention to William and Silvee.

The dining room looked formal, too: three violinists playing romantic music . . . bouquets of red roses on the tables . . . waiters in black tuxedos. Even the Funners looked like little ladies and gentlemen in their best outfits.

At their table, Fernando presented them with huge menus, and it occurred to Melanie that he might be in on the drug smuggling, too. Maybe every staff and crew member was in on it! No, that was impossible. Still, maybe. . . .

———

After dinner, the first seating's passengers returned to the Ruby Lounge for the evening's entertainment. Melanie and the TCCers scrambled for the best seating area, right across from the stage and microphone.

After they'd settled, Melanie spoke quietly. "Guys, there's been jewelry stolen from the ship's safe, too."

"It has to be an inside job," Cara said. "Someone working behind the registration desk . . . maybe Ted who gave Melanie and me the supply room key."

"Exactly what I've been thinking," Melanie said.

"Why should we worry about jewelry being stolen?" Jess

asked. "Isn't that the security person's job?"

After a long discussion, they decided it definitely was not their job, unless they could help find the culprit.

"The same goes for the drug smuggling," Cara said.

Melanie shrugged. "I don't know about that. I've been thinking, it's almost as if God arranged for us to be behind the disco curtain just then."

"God?" Cara echoed. "God arranged it?"

It occurred to Melanie this was the first time they'd even considered Him. "Let's pray about it," she suggested.

Tricia nodded. "Let's pray now . . . for God's will for us. Melanie, why don't you start the prayer?"

Melanie felt uneasy about praying aloud since she'd only become a Christian this summer. "Dear Heavenly Father," she began. "We're not so sure of what to do. . . ."

When they said "Amen," she looked up and found at least a dozen of their youth room Funners settling around them and listening.

"We want to sit with you," Hannah said.

"Can we?" Sarah implored. "You're more fun than parents. Can we? Can we?"

Melanie looked at the other TCCers, and they all nodded. "If you'll behave," she told the kids.

"We will," Hannah said. "We will! We promise!"

Surprisingly, they all behaved well through Maxwell Thornton's opening song. He sang "I've Got to Be Me" so dramatically that it was clear he considered himself *a very important person.*

Next was a dance number.

When the magician came onstage, the kids sat up on their knees to watch. Then two of the boys ran onstage to check out the tricks, and Melanie rushed after them and dragged them back. The magician smiled, but he was *not* pleased. The interruption messed up his trick.

Still, if that was the only trouble the Funners caused, Melanie decided that she could survive it.

CHAPTER

8

*O*ut on the deck in the moonlight, they'd composed the FAX as simply as possible, hoping it wouldn't raise suspicions.

Mr. Smith, c/o Mr. & Mrs. Bennett,
c/o Mr. & Mrs. McColl
Cruise exciting with interesting older people, but not right without you. It's high time you join us for a great round-up. Tricia Bennett.

They'd decided that an FBI man like Mr. Smith would know he was needed from the words "not right without you."

"Exciting with interesting older people" hinted that the older Hermanns were aboard ship.

"A great round-up" meant that someone or something needed to be caught. In fact, it could mean both. And "high time" meant drugs were aboard!

Since just recently Mr. Smith had been involved with catching the Hermanns in drug money laundering, it seemed certain he'd know that Tricia's FAX concerned drugs, too.

This morning, as they ate breakfast on the deck, no answer to the FAX had been received.

Melanie swallowed the last bite of blueberry muffin. "Are you sure they sent it?"

"Positive," Tricia answered. "I stood at the registration desk and watched Ted send it. On top of that, he gave me the FAX receipt to show it was received at Jess's home FAX."

Ted was the one in charge of the keys, Melanie remembered. So he sent FAXes—and maybe other communications. Probably he wasn't the only person on the ship to send them, though.

"It was my home FAX, all right," Jess assured them, "and I know everyone's home now." She looked around to be sure no one could hear. "What I've been thinking is that the FBI must know the Hermanns are on this cruise. They probably keep an eye on people who get out of jail on insufficient evidence . . . trying to get more evidence on them. It makes sense."

Melanie glanced around herself, then whispered, "You mean FBI people might already be on this cruise ship?"

Jess shrugged. "Maybe. I wouldn't be surprised."

"How can we find out?" Melanie asked.

"That's the big question," Tricia said. "They try to stay undercover. But so do drug smugglers."

Melanie drew a deep breath. "Then the biggest question

might be 'How do we know who's FBI and who's doing the drug smuggling?' "

"That's the biggest question, all right," Becky answered. "That's the very biggest question."

Moments later, Maxwell Thornton approached their umbrella table, his face grim. "I hope you girls realize you should never have let those boys interfere with the magician last night. It nearly ruined his act. From now on, the youth room will be open every night after dinner. It's apparently best to keep kids and our evening programs separated."

Melanie protested, "But we were only supposed to take care of Santa Rosita kids, not all of the kids on the entire ship—"

"There are no *buts* about this," he said. "And I don't want you wandering around to supply closets and such. Keep in mind that I am the cruise director on this ship."

When he left, Cara asked Melanie and Jess, "Who knew you went to the supply closet?"

"Ted," Melanie answered. "And come to think of it, Karla and Jason Hermann and the other kids! We said we were going for supplies before we left!"

Someone on the deck shouted, "Antigua! There's Antigua!"

Sure enough, the green island of Antigua glistened in the distance, and Auntie Ying-Ying already stood at the rail with her camcorder panning the scenery.

As the *Golden Isle* approached the island, buses and taxis assembled to take them on island tours. Before long, passengers disembarked from the ship. Walking down the metal gangway, Melanie saw they'd have to ride on the same bus as the Hermanns, who were already climbing aboard.

Auntie Ying-Ying didn't recognize them and climbed on the bus right behind them.

When Melanie got on the bus, she saw the front seat was vacant. "All right! We can sit up front!" she called back to her friends. "Oops . . . there's a 'reserved' sign on it. Guess we sit farther back."

When everyone was settled on their bus, the black driver turned from his seat. "Good day," he said with a clipped British accent. "My name is Martin, and I bid you welcome to the city of St. John's in Antigua. Your regular guide is sick today, but we have a replacement, a man who knows our island inside out."

Maxwell Thornton climbed onto the bus. Smiling at the driver, he said, "I'm elected to do the tour guiding today."

The driver gave a laugh. "So I heard. And so I told our passengers."

Maxwell settled on the reserved front seat.

Melanie whispered to Jess, "How did we get so lucky?"

Jess shrugged.

The driver started the bus and they took off from the ship parking lot. As they rode through the city's traffic, Maxwell spoke into the microphone. "St. John's is the capital and major city of the island of Antigua. Columbus visited here, as did Sir Francis Drake and many famous pirates."

From the back of the bus, Sid Hermann asked, "They still have pirates around?"

Maxwell laughed. "The only pirates are shopkeepers trying to get the tourists' money."

Everyone chuckled, but it occurred to Melanie that drug smugglers were just as bad as the old pirates.

When the city of St. John's was behind them, they drove through green countryside and small villages with names like All Saints and Liberta. In the villages, every house seemed to have at least one dense tree with big leaves and round, green fruit bigger than grapefruit.

"Breadfruit," Maxwell explained. "People here fry breadfruit and mash it and eat it every which way."

They drove along through the countryside, past cotton fields and sugarcane plantations. On the road, barebacked native boys rode scrawny donkeys, and some carried enormous bunches of bananas on their heads.

"Looks to me," Melanie remarked to Jess, "like we're in the pages of *National Geographic*."

They stopped at a plantation house where English royalty had visited. Next came Lord Nelson's Dockyard with lots of boats, then a musty naval museum, which William called "very, very interesting."

For lunch, they stopped at Admiral's Inn, an old brick restaurant with outdoor tables and chairs. Auntie Ying-Ying handed Melanie the camcorder. "You take video pictures. I take Silvee to rest room. You push button here for zoom. You know already."

Melanie nodded, examining the camera to remember.

As she panned the scene, the camcorder's viewfinder brought Maxwell and Sid Hermann into focus. Just to the side of the restaurant, they spoke privately to each other. Curious, Melanie zoomed in on them, and it looked as if their faces were just inches away. Backing off, she saw Sid Hermann pass a black briefcase to Maxwell. *Money? Drug money?* She caught the exchange on the video tape, just in case. Luckily, they didn't seem to notice.

After lunch, their bus returned to the *Golden Isle*. Still carrying the black briefcase, Maxwell made arrangements with several taxi drivers to wait. "Some of the passengers want to get into their bathing suits, then go out to Buccaneer Cove," he told them.

"We wait," the drivers answered with musical voices. "We be waiting fo' you."

Melanie glanced at the ship. She whispered to Becky, "Look, they're bringing crates of fruit and all kinds of stuff onto the ship."

Becky looked at the scene with her. "Wonder if that's how they smuggle the drugs on."

Melanie nodded. "Could be." Suddenly an idea struck. "The coffins! What if they smuggle the drugs in coffins? Inspectors at customs wouldn't open them because they'd expect bodies to be in there."

"Yuck!" Jess shuddered. "What an awful thought!"

Later, at Buccaneer Cove, a native band pounded out a calypso beat on steel drums, and the TCCers settled on the beach. Foamy waves drifted into the white sandy cove, and Melanie couldn't wait to swim out with her friends.

As she headed for the water, Maxwell appeared at her side. "Did you take my picture this morning?" he demanded.

"I . . . took pictures of the scenery. Why would I take pictures of you?" She saw Auntie Ying-Ying videotaping them now. Gaining courage, Melanie added, "I know you're a very important man on the ship, but are you *that* important, Mr. Thornton?"

He eyed her, then Auntie Ying-Ying, with annoyance and sauntered away.

Now they had video evidence that Maxwell and Sid Hermann knew each other well enough to pass a briefcase between them. And they had a tape of Maxwell questioning her! Maybe it'd be best not to tell anyone about the videos now.

Melanie ran out and dove into the warm turquoise water.

———————

That night in the youth rooms, the ship's Funners worked on their costumes again. Other artwork on colored construction paper went up on the corridor windows to keep outsiders from peering in.

Later, the TCCers met on the back of the Promenade Deck in the moonlight again.

"No answer to my FAX," Tricia said. "No reply from Mr. Smith, either. Not even anything from Jess's or my parents."

"Are you sure the FAX was sent?" Melanie asked again.

"Positive," Tricia insisted. "I don't see how Ted could have faked it."

Melanie shook her head. "I'm beginning to wonder if what Jess and I saw and heard in the disco was our imaginations."

"No way," Jess said. "We couldn't both have imagined it. It was real, all right."

———————

The next day the ship stopped at the island of Barbados—their third stop already. Shimmering in the morning sun, its city of Bridgetown revealed docks, warehouses, government buildings, and roads with snarled traffic. Maxwell was already telling about Barbados on the ship's loudspeakers. *"Unlike our first two islands, here civilization has unfortunately set in."*

As the *Golden Isle* docked, the pier did look a mess—a busy mess. Lines of trucks waited to unload and load the ship. The first two islands had seemed so simple and innocent that it made her wonder if maybe this one was the drug stop.

Maxwell still spoke over the loudspeakers. *"One of the highlights of Barbados is Sam Lord's Castle on the other side of the island. Sam Lord was a pirate with elegant taste, so you'll find his castle most interesting."*

Melanie remarked to Tricia. "I think old Maxwell is a pirate with elegant taste himself."

Then she added, "Still no word from Mr. Smith?"

"Nothing," Tricia answered. "Absolutely nothing. I asked at the registration desk again, and Ted looked at me as if he were getting suspicious."

"Let's hope not," Melanie said. "You'd think if the FBI had someone on the ship, they'd have contacted us by now. Of course, they wouldn't know that Jess and I saw three of the culprits in the disco."

"Maybe they're waiting until we're back under U.S. control—you know, at St. Thomas or Puerto Rico."

Steffi hurried over to them. "Ready for a big day, girls?"

"Ready as we'll ever be," Tricia answered cheerily. It sounded as if they didn't have a care in the world.

Steffi smiled, her teeth white against her deep tan. "I think you guys are enjoying the trip, even though you're saddled with all of those kids. You're having a great adventure, aren't you?"

"We are," Melanie agreed. "In fact, we talked about that last night. Despite so many kids, we wouldn't have traded this trip for anything. Of course, the kids' movies and the bridge tour make things easier for us. But the kids are great. We just have to have a good attitude."

They visited for quite a while before Melanie found the courage to ask the question. "You wouldn't know a . . . special Mr. Smith, would you?"

Steffi blinked. "No. No 'special' Mr. Smith. Why?"

"Oh, nothing," Tricia assured her.

"Is he a passenger?" Steffi asked. "We usually have several Smiths aboard ship every week."

Melanie shook her head. Somehow she'd thought that Steffi might know more than she let on. "It's nothing . . . nothing important." Melanie turned toward the rail. "Whoa, we're almost docked already! Time is flying too fast. Way too fast."

Steffi glanced down at the pier with her. "Time does seem to fly faster as the cruise moves on, doesn't it? I'm so glad you girls are aboard. You've made the trip lots of fun for the younger kids."

Moments later, Auntie Ying-Ying, Silvee, and William appeared. As usual, Melanie's aunt talked the most, and for a change, Melanie was grateful.

That day and the next day on the island of Martinique sped by, but Melanie kept a sharp eye out for coffins being carried on or off the ship. No sign of coffins. Not much time left on the cruise, either. Only the island of St. Thomas before they returned to Puerto Rico. Only two more days of cruising.

That night, when the other TCCers started a Magic Carpet Ride to Martinique, Melanie told Jess, "I think we should go back to the supply closet, no matter what."

"When?" Jess asked, alarmed.

"Now's as good a time as any," Melanie decided.

The ship's Funners had their eyes closed for the Magic Carpet Ride. Melanie glanced at Karla and Jason. Eyes closed, both of them.

"This very moment!" Melanie told Jess.

They ran for the door, opening it and closing it quietly. The corridor was empty.

"Let's take the steps down," Jess said. "Hurry before they miss us in the youth rooms."

They raced down the steps.

"The supply closet key?" Jess asked.

Melanie shook her head. "No, we don't want to alert Ted or anyone else. We go straight to the disco. Eight o'clock . . . it won't be open for dancing yet."

Out of breath but unseen, they reached the Ocean Deck. There was the closet door with the sign that said SUPPLY CLOSET, CREW ONLY. And there was the disco door, to the right down the corridor.

Melanie tried the knob. Unlocked.

She opened the door slowly and peered in.

The same as before: black curtains circling the room . . . the large mirrored ball hanging from the ceiling . . . one bare light bulb near the cargo door. Now the engine noise seemed even louder.

Jess whispered, "No one's here."

"Let's check for the coffins," Melanie said.

They glanced behind the black curtains. *Nothing!*

"Bet they're in the cargo area," Melanie answered. She pointed straight ahead to the cargo door. "In there."

"Let's try it," Jess said.

Slowly, they eased open the cargo door.

Crates and boxes filled the dimly lit room, some piled to the ceiling. Melanie glanced from one end to the other of the cargo hold and spotted the coffins near the big outside doors. She whispered, "There are the coffins."

"Kids!" a man yelled from the other side. "Hey! What're you doin' lookin' in here! Someone didn't lock the disco door—"

Melanie slammed the cargo hold door behind them. They raced through the disco, slamming that door behind them, too, and ran on through the Ocean Deck corridor. The cargo hold was so crowded, it'd take a while for anyone to get through it.

As they rounded the corner, the elevator doors were about to close. "Quick, get on it!" Jess said, sticking her hand in to stop them. "Come on!"

The elevator doors closed, then the elevator rose with them aboard.

"Safe," Melanie said. "We're safe! At least for now."

She caught her breath. "Guess I should tell you that back in Antigua I videoed Sid Hermann giving Maxwell a black briefcase."

"Whoa!" Jess exclaimed. "Evidence they know each other! Evidence they're working together!"

Melanie nodded. "Yep. I played the video on our cabin TV, and it's perfect. Guess we'd better hang on to it."

She prayed without closing her eyes, *Please give us peace in the middle of this mess, too!*

CHAPTER

9

Sunday morning, the TCCers and Melanie's family attended the church service in the ship's theater. As they sat down, Melanie was amazed to see Karla and Jason seated in the second row with their grandmother.

"Whoa, look at that!" Tricia said, motioning at the Hermanns. "I prayed for them the time I baby-sat!"

After the service, Karla, Jason, and their grandmother lingered up front to talk to the minister.

As they passed, Mrs. Hermann was saying, "Jason and Karla's grandfather doesn't come to church with me, so it's nice to have the children along today. I try to take them to church whenever I can. It's good for them."

So that's why God had Tricia baby-sit for them, Melanie thought. *Maybe even why He had the TCCers on the cruise! Their grandmother must be praying for them!*

Suddenly Melanie felt guilty for not wanting to look after these kids. They might be rich on the outside, but they sure were poor on the inside.

They left the theater, then went up to the Promenade Deck. Outside, someone yelled, "There's St. Thomas!"

Sure enough, the green island of St. Thomas rose from the sea in the distance, and nine white cruise ships gleamed at its docks. Maxwell was already speaking over the ship's loudspeakers, calling St. Thomas "a shopper's paradise."

"You can spend the whole day there looking for bargains on just about everything," he announced. *"Or if history is more to your liking, visit Blackbeard's Tower overlooking St. Thomas Bay. Old Blackbeard, the pirate, made his headquarters there."*

Auntie Ying-Ying videotaped the hilly island as the *Golden Isle* approached. After filming the harbor's yachts and white cruise ships, she turned off her camcorder. "You girls ready for costume party tonight? What you be?"

Melanie jabbered, "Everyone's going to be a pirate. You'd think there'd be a clown or two, or maybe a princess, but, no, everyone wants to be pirates. We brought clown suits along, but the kids talked us into being part of the Eye-patch Pirate Gang."

Auntie Ying-Ying turned to Silvee. "You pirate, too?"

Silvee nodded with certainty. "Me too."

William put on his disappointed voice. "Just like all of us *have* to go on the Coral World Island Tour."

"Listen, William, we have been working hard for this cruise," Melanie told him. "And Auntie Ying-Ying had to buy your ticket—"

He slashed a karate kick at her. "Hiii-ee-yah!"

Melanie jumped back. "Stop that kicking!" She turned away, raised her chin indignantly, and watched the ship dock. Tourists, taxis, and buses crowded the area as the dock workers caught the *Golden Isle*'s mooring lines. Just then, Maxwell appeared on deck, and Auntie Ying-Ying called out, "Like to take you picture, Mr. Thornton."

Maxwell gave her his phony ear-to-ear smile. "I'm honored, Mrs. Lin. Where do you want me? With St. Thomas as the background? The other ships as the background? As the cruise director, I'm very accustomed to posing for our passengers, as you might suspect."

Yech, what a bragger! Melanie thought.

"St. Thomas in back," Auntie replied. "Move right, please, Mr. Thornton."

"Yes, ma'am," Maxwell replied, stretching his smile.

"Girls, you get in picture, too," Auntie directed. "You wear very colorful outfits today."

Melanie saw Maxwell's smile fade, and she followed his gaze. Nearby, Sid Hermann sat in a deck chair, glaring at Maxwell. If looks could kill, Sid Hermann's expression was pure poison.

Maxwell stuttered, "M-maybe I'd better get to my duties. Can we finish another time, Mrs. Lin. . . ?"

But Auntie already had her camcorder on him. "Is fine, Mr. Maxwell. Just need one more big smile."

Maxwell pulled another phony smile, then nodded nervously. "If you'll excuse me . . . I'm sorry—"

"No problem, no problem," Auntie assured him. "Have many good pictures of you already. Important job, cruise director."

Despite her nervousness, Melanie had to bite down on her lips to keep from laughing.

As Maxwell hurried off, William mimicked, "Important

job, cruise director." He flung out a wilder than ever karate kick. "Hiii-ee-yah!"

"William!" Melanie yelled. "You're going to hurt someone, kicking like that!"

"William," Auntie said, "enough karate."

Before long, Maxwell spoke on the loudspeakers again, calling passengers for the tours. After a while, he said, *"The Coral World Island Tour should now disembark. Coral World Island Tour. Please meet your tour leader down on the dock."*

The TCCers' white sandals clattered on the ship's metal gangway. "Last tour, guys," Tricia reminded them.

"I hate to see the cruise end," Melanie admitted. "I didn't dream it'd be such fun—even with sitting so many kids." They climbed on the open trams and soon rode along in the island's balmy breeze.

Since each island had been so different, Melanie felt disappointed to see Coral World was similar to Sea World in San Diego. Still, the coral and colorful fish were beautiful.

Just before noon, they returned to the ship, and Melanie felt troubled again. As they walked up the gangway, the ship's bells rang, and the familiar words came, *"Lunch is now served."*

Auntie Ying-Ying said, "Silvee, William, and I eat down in the dining room. Too hot outside on deck."

"Not for us," Melanie told her.

Auntie laughed. "You go then."

The TCCers hurried straight to the Promenade Deck, saved an umbrella table, then headed for the nearby buffet. The aromas of fried chicken, sausages, meatballs, fish, lasagna, and spaghetti wafted from enormous serving dishes.

Their trays full, they returned to their table. Despite her

uneasiness, Melanie admired the view of St. Thomas while they ate. This afternoon they'd go to the shopping area—

Her gaze stopped on a familiar face at a nearby umbrella table. The man wore dark sunglasses, but she'd definitely seen him somewhere before . . . somewhere near home. . . .

"Don't look," she told the TCCers. "It's Mr. Smith!"

They asked, almost in unison, "Where?"

She forced her eyes down to the food in her plate. "Don't look. He probably doesn't want anyone to know he's here. He's at the middle table by the pool. Tricia, he knows you better than the rest of us. Maybe you should meander over there. Act like you've left your sunglasses or something there near him."

Tricia nodded, her reddish blond hair bobbing over her shoulders. "Okay. Eat up, guys. Let's hope I can still act!"

When they left the ship for town, Melanie asked Tricia, "What did he say?"

"First he said, 'Keep walking.' Then he said, 'See you in the Little Switzerland shop at two o'clock. Linens department. Just you.' "

"Was anyone watching you two?" Jess asked.

"No one," Tricia answered. "Believe me, I checked."

Once they were in the shopping area, Melanie said, "Shopping here would be fun, but I'm so hyper about Mr. Smith . . . not to mention Maxwell and Sid Hermann."

Luckily, tourists jammed the streets and shops. Shoppers were so busy bargain hunting that the TCCers might as well have been invisible.

No sign of Maxwell, nor of the Hermanns.

Just before two o'clock, the TCCers headed through the blue doors of Little Switzerland. It was a big shop.

When they reached the perfume area, Tricia suggested, "Hang around here, guys. See if anyone's watching us. A good thing the store is crowded."

They tried to be low-profile, sampling perfumes.

Tricia glanced at her watch. "Two o'clock now. See you guys. Better meet out front."

They sampled perfumes until a saleswomen stopped by a second time and asked, "Are you *sure* I can't help you girls?"

They headed outside, and before long, Tricia met them in front of the ship. "Come on, guys," she said.

Moving along, Melanie whispered, "Was he there?"

Tricia nodded. "Can't talk about it yet."

Worried, Melanie glanced around. Still no Hermanns to be seen, nor anyone watching the TCCers.

Finally, they found a quiet place at the end of an alley.

Tricia said, "Mr. Smith understood our coded messages in the FAX, but he didn't want to FAX us back in case the message got into the wrong hands. He said it was all he could do to keep our parents from flying here! But he's had two people on the ship working with him, and they were watching out for us. That's why he held off until he was sure the drugs were really aboard."

―――――

On the *Golden Isle*, Melanie worried through dinner, then in the youth rooms as everyone dressed in pirate costumes. Karla and Jason Hermann were the only Funners not in the costume night program. Karla had said her grand-

120

father didn't want them parading around as murderous pirates. He thought "it looked bad."

Melanie, Jess, Cara, and Becky, wearing pirates' costumes, waited with the costumed Funners behind the dark stage curtain to the Ruby Lounge. Everyone wore black—hats, clothes, and eye patches. Some carried gray plastic swords. Melanie thought her girl pirates—Sarah, Hannah, and Silvee—looked sweet. But William, Kip, Jake, and Bunky made up for them with fierceness.

With God's help, the TCCers had sat all these kids on the ship! That part was perfect. If only Tricia weren't meeting Mr. Smith again right now.

On stage, a costumed "princess" sashayed across the stage, showing off sparkling jewelry. When the "princess" finished, the audience applauded politely.

Maxwell did not sound quite so confident as he announced, "Here comes the biggest, scariest band of pirates you've ever seen! Let's hear some applause for the Twelve Candles Club girls and our junior cruisers!"

The ship's orchestra broke into a hearty pirate song.

Doing backward flips, pirate Jess led the smaller pirates onto the stage. They all wore eye patches and carried paper cutlasses in their mouths. William led the bigger pirate boys, karate chopping as they ran across the stage.

Everyone sang loudly, "Oh, it's the pirate's life for me! It's the pirate's life for me. . . !"

Next, Cara came with her pirates, snaking onto the stage behind the others. Then Becky and her pirates . . .

Where is Tricia? Melanie wondered.

Suddenly Tricia rushed up in her pirate's outfit, wisps of her reddish blond hair from under the black pirate's hat giving her away. A tall pirate followed her.

"Who's that?" Melanie asked.

Tricia whispered, "Mr. Smith in disguise! Maxwell has agreed to tell everything—"

"Maxwell confessed?!" Melanie exclaimed.

Tricia nodded, grabbing her black crepe paper pirate's hat before it fell off. "Just before he went on stage. Those are FBI people sitting at the table closest to him. They've got plenty of evidence on him, but they're letting him do his *last* show. Your aunt let them see the video of Sid giving Maxwell the briefcase. It was full of money! One big problem: Sid Hermann reboarded the ship in St. Thomas, and now he's disappeared! They've checked cabins, decks, lifeboats—"

"Who's 'they'?"

"Mr. Smith and Steffi and Ted—"

"Steffi and Ted?!" Melanie echoed.

Tricia nodded. "They've been helping the FBI. That's partly why Maxwell's confessing—anything to save his skin. He's even admitted stealing jewelry from the ship's safe to support his drug habit! And he says the man in charge of the kitchen is involved, too. He's blabbing like mad."

Melanie drew a breath. "When you think about it, it's probably not too surprising, his looking out for himself first."

Suddenly an idea struck. "Whoa! Did you tell them about the coffins in the cargo hold by the disco?"

"No, but I'm sure they checked there, too."

Onstage, the orchestra played another chorus of the pirate music, and Maxwell asked over the microphone,

"Where're our other pirates? We think there're more pirates on this ship."

"Yo, ho, ho! Let's go!" Melanie called out, leading her pirates out far behind Becky's group. "Yo, ho, ho! It's the pirate's life for me. . . ."

She glanced ahead. Jess's group streamed into the audience. Melanie let out a loud, "Yo, ho, ho! Yo, ho, ho!" and waved her band of pirates to follow.

Leading them around the stage, her mind spun, too. Sid Hermann had to be in the cargo hold with those coffins. He could easily hide among the barrels and cartons.

Behind her, Tricia's band of pirates burst onto the stage with a mighty, "Yo, ho, ho!" The audience laughed and applauded the endless pirates streaming across the stage, then weaving among them through the Ruby Lounge. Steffi, dressed in a pirate's costume, too, wove along with them.

Melanie glanced back at the last pirate. Mr. Smith was still with them. He probably thought his pirate's outfit offered a good chance to check out the audience as the snaked through them with the other pirates.

Still no Sid Hermann.

Suddenly Melanie knew exactly what to do.

"Come on, pirates! We're going to parade through the ship. Let's hear some good yo-ho-ho's!"

"Yo, ho, ho!" they yelled. "Yo, ho, ho!"

The orchestra's music faded as she led her pirates out of the Ruby Lounge and toward the stairwell. "Yo, ho, ho! Down to the Ocean Deck!"

Starting down the stairs, she glanced back. Her pirates followed, and here came Tricia's group, still singing and yo-ho-hoing. The ship rolled, but they only laughed and hung on to the stairway banisters. Pirate Steffi reeled along with them at the end of the line.

Melanie led them down one deck, then another and another until they were finally on the Ocean Deck. The familiar DISCO sign pointed the way. Ted stood unlocking the disco door when, to his amazement, they yo-ho-hoed past him into the disco. Melanie tried the cargo hold door. Locked.

"Yo, ho, ho, Ted!" she called out over the roar of the ship's engines. "We need to get in here. Sid has to be there."

From the back of the line, Mr. Smith yelled, "Open it!"

Ted hurried forward to unlock the door.

Once the door was open, Melanie called back, "Mateys, watch for no-good guys in the disco!" Then she rushed behind Mr. Smith into the hold. Ted, Steffi, and the other TCCers followed.

The cargo hold was as dimly lit as the other time she saw it, but not as jammed with crates and cartons.

"Yo, ho, ho!" the Funners sang out as they made their way through the disco room.

In the cargo hold, she squeezed through the crates, barrels, and cartons until she neared the big cargo door.

Eight coffins stood by the door!

Eight coffins ready to be unloaded—and who'd think to look for drugs in coffins?

But no sign of Sid Hermann. Only cargo piled all the way to the ceiling.

She edged over through the crates and cartons to the coffins.

No, it couldn't be what she was thinking, but she'd have to try.

She ran her fingers under the first coffin's overlapping lid. Nothing unusual. She was surprised to be able to lift the lid. It was full of bricks of green-wrapped stuff!

Just like they showed on TV.

Drugs!

Mr. Smith rushed over while she moved to the next coffin and opened the lid. More drugs! The next held drugs too! Seven coffins full! Someone hadn't nailed the lids down yet.

At the eighth coffin, she felt something different under the overlapping lid.

Air holes!

"This is it!" she shouted over the engine noise. "This has to be it! He has to be in here!"

Lord, help me, she prayed and threw back the lid.

Sid Hermann alive as ever—and furious.

Melanie felt rooted to the floor as, red with fury, he climbed out.

"Why didn't you idiots nail the lids down?" he yelled before he saw his cohorts weren't there.

Mr. Smith yelled, "We've got you this time, Hermann! Get your hands up!"

Sid Hermann raised his hands, then with a swift movement, toppled cartons toward Ted and Mr. Smith.

Melanie jumped back, alone behind Sid Hermann as he reached in his pocket for what must surely be a gun.

Peace flooded her spirit, and suddenly she knew what to do. "Hiii-ee-yah!" she yelled, kicking the back of Sid Hermann's knees.

He crumpled.

Ted, Mr. Smith, and two other FBI men burst from behind the cartons and grabbed him.

Mr. Smith said, "Guess we'll have to tie you up, like they did the old Caribbean pirates, Hermann." He turned to Melanie. "Get the kids out of here and back up to the lounge! Thanks for your help!"

For an instant, Melanie heard only the ship's engines. She recalled praying for an exciting cruise—but to be peaceful in the midst of it. Her prayers had sure been answered.

The next instant, she ran into the disco with a "Yo, ho, ho! Yo, ho, ho!"

The "pirates" waved their swords in the air as they followed her through the door and back to the stairway. The kids must have thought this was all a game, and they didn't need to know that Sid Hermann was a *real* bad guy!

At the entrance to the lounge, the TCC pirates and Pirate William hung back.

Jess, Cara, Becky, and Tricia turned to Melanie with amazement. "We didn't know you knew karate!"

Melanie straightened her pirate's hat. "I didn't. It's just that when you have a brother like William, you can't help learning something about it. Besides, suddenly I knew what I had to do—"

"Yeah!" William cheered. "Let's hear it for karate!"

Melanie and the other TCCers gazed back at him.

She'd tell her friends, Auntie, William, and Silvee about the Lord's help later. Right now, she and the other TCCers assumed karate stances, then chopped the air toward him.

He ran.

"Hiii-ee-yah!" they shouted after him, trying not to laugh. "Hiii-ee-yah!"

When Lily Vanessa Shields arrives in the TCCers' neighborhood, she gets roped into singing a solo for their Youth Sunday at church and helping pet-sit Cat Woman's yard full of animals, which includes a fierce goat.

With her gangly features and dark skin, Lily stands out from the club members. What will she have to do to be accepted?

Find out in the eleventh book of THE TWELVE CANDLES CLUB. Don't miss it!